Acting Edition

Twelve Angry Men: A Musical

Music and Lyrics by
Michael Holland

Book by
David Simpatico

Adapted from the play by
Reginald Rose

concord
theatricals

FOR PRODUCTION INQUIRIES

UNITED STATES AND CANADA
info@concordtheatricals.com
1-866-979-0447

UNITED KINGDOM AND EUROPE
licensing@concordtheatricals.co.uk
020-7054-7298

Each title is subject to availability from Concord Theatricals Corp., depending upon country of performance. Please be aware that *TWELVE ANGRY MEN: A MUSICAL* may not be licensed by Concord Theatricals Corp. in your territory. Professional and amateur producers should contact the nearest Concord Theatricals Corp. office or licensing partner to verify availability.

No one shall make any changes in this title(s) for the purpose of production. No part of this book may be reproduced, stored in a retrieval system, scanned, uploaded, or transmitted in any form, by any means, now known or yet to be invented, including mechanical, electronic, digital, photocopying, recording, videotaping, or otherwise, without the prior written permission of the publisher. No one shall share this title(s), or any part of this title(s), through any social media or file hosting websites.

For all inquiries regarding motion picture, television, online/digital and other media rights, please contact Concord Theatricals Corp.

THIRD-PARTY MATERIALS USE NOTE

Licensees are solely responsible for obtaining formal written permission from copyright owners to use copyrighted third-party materials (e.g., incidental music not provided in connection with a performance license, artworks, logos) in the performance of this play and are strongly cautioned to do so. If no such permission is obtained by the licensee, then the licensee must use only original materials and materials that the licensee owns and controls. Licensees are solely responsible and liable for clearances of all third-party copyrighted materials, and shall indemnify the copyright owners of the play(s) and their licensing agent, Concord Theatricals Corp., against any costs, expenses, losses and liabilities arising from the use of such copyrighted third-party materials by licensees. For music, please contact the appropriate music licensing authority in your territory for the rights to any incidental music not provided in connection with a performance license.

IMPORTANT BILLING AND CREDIT REQUIREMENTS

If you have obtained performance rights to this title, please refer to your licensing agreement for important billing and credit requirements.

TWELVE ANGRY MEN: A MUSICAL was first produced by Theater Latté Da (Peter Rothstein, Founding Artistic Director; Elisa Spencer-Kaplan, Managing Director), Minneapolis, Minnesota, and had its world premiere there on June 11, 2022. The performance was directed by Peter Rothstein, with music direction by Denise Prosek, choreography by Kelli Foster Warder, scenic design by Benjamin Olsen, costume design by Matthew LeFebvre, lighting design by Paul Whitaker, sound design by Nicholas Tranby, associate music direction by Russ Kaplan, orchestrations by Michael Holland, and dramaturgy by Elissa Adams. The production stage manager was Z Makila. The cast was as follows:

FOREMAN (JUROR NUMBER 1) . . . . Matt Riehle

JUROR NUMBER 2 . . . . Riley McNutt

JUROR NUMBER 3 . . . . Charlie Clark

JUROR NUMBER 4 . . . . Sasha Andreev

JUROR NUMBER 5 . . . . Brian Kim McCormick

JUROR NUMBER 6 . . . . Adan Varela

JUROR NUMBER 7 . . . . Wariboko Semenitari

JUROR NUMBER 8 . . . . Curtis Bannister

JUROR NUMBER 9 . . . . T Mychael Rambo

JUROR NUMBER 10 . . . . James Michael Detmar

JUROR NUMBER 11 . . . . Bradley Greenwald

JUROR NUMBER 12 . . . . Reese Britts

CHARACTERS

FOREMAN (JUROR NUMBER 1) – 30s; solid, working man; high school assistant football coach in Queens; takes his duties seriously, wants to do a good job; Caucasian

JUROR NUMBER 2 – 20–30s; bank teller; excited about the jury process; Caucasian

JUROR NUMBER 3 – 40–50s; bullish, gruff, passionate; a bulwark of a man; owns a messenger service; very excitable; high voice/short fuse; Caucasian

JUROR NUMBER 4 – 40s; stock broker; analytical to a fault; rational; buttoned up; does not sweat; Caucasian

JUROR NUMBER 5 – 20s; male nurse, on the shy side; lives and works in Harlem; Korean American

JUROR NUMBER 6 – 30s; blue collar; house painter; plain-spoken, genuine; respects his elders; Mexican American

JUROR NUMBER 7 – 20s; marmalade salesman; snappy, sporty guy; always ready with a joke; big Yankees fan, has tickets to a game tonight; African American

JUROR NUMBER 8 – 30s; architect; rational, empathetic, compassionate and unsatisfied with the evidence; a brand new daddy of a six-month-old baby boy; African American

JUROR NUMBER 9 – 68; retired; congenial, inquisitive; 20/20 vision; does not suffer fools gladly; African American

JUROR NUMBER 10 – 40s–50s; coarse, belligerent, entertaining; owns several commercial garages; has a bad summer cold and a bad opinion of anyone different from himself; Caucasian

JUROR NUMBER 11 – 40s; soft-spoken; keen mind; polite; watchmaker; Middle European, post-war immigrant; Caucasian

JUROR NUMBER 12 – 30s; bright-eyed ad man; talks in slogans; amiable; his opinion flip-flops with the force of argument; African American/mixed race

SETTING

The Jury Room of a New York City Court of Law.

TIME

Summer, 1959

AUTHORS' NOTES

Reginald Rose's *Twelve Angry Men* has been part of the American cultural fabric for decades. Our adaptation process has been to musicalize and calibrate the connection between this wonderful, incisive play, and the world we live in now. We began by integrating the all-white cast of the original script with a mix of non-white characters who connect the play to our current, multi-cultural world. This allowed us to incorporate nuances that filter our current age through the 1950s setting. Musically, we went full throttle with the toxic masculinity already present in the play, and found its musical expression in the swagger of late 1950s post-Bop jazz. The harmonies are dissonant and tense, the feeling sparse and jittery, which perfectly suits the themes of rage, father/son issues, racism, ageism, and the American judicial system. The music and dialogue bubble up out of one another as the men, who are diverse in their class, educational levels, and ethnicities, converge and interact. Despite their differences, they arrive at a peaceful resolution of their conflicts, providing us with the hope that we, too, can do the same.

MUSICAL NUMBERS

01. Voir Dire . . . . Company
02. The Oath. . . . . Company
03. Hottest Day of the Year . . . . .Company
04. The Very Least. . . . . Number 8
05. Once Around the Table . . . . .Company
06. Ask Me If I Care . . . . Number 3
07. Never Too Easy . . . . .Company
08. Know What I Mean . . . . .Number 10
09. Lights Out . . . . Number 8
10. Just Words . . . . .Company
11. Coincidence . . . . .Number 4 & Company
12. Somewhere Between Now and Then. . . . . .Number 9
13. The Big Idea. . . . . .Company
14. Raindrops. . . . . Number 11
15. Killing You . . . . .Numbers 3, 5, 8 & Company
16. Strike Three . . . . .Numbers 7 & 11
17. What I Meant . . . . .Number 10
18. The Only One Who Sees . . . . .Company
19. Hopefully Not Too Late . . . . .Number 8 & Company
20. Evensong. . . . . .Company

[MUSIC NO. 01 – VOIR DIRE]

(Twelve empty chairs face the audience, a jury box waiting to be filled. Sound effect: a ticking clock.)

*(One by one, twelve **JURORS** take their chairs in pools of light, as they engage in the interview during the jury selection process.)*

*(We begin with **NUMBER 2**, who sits forward, listening to a question, and replies. Music begins under the scene while the men speak.)*

NUMBER 2. Yes, a bank clerk; oh, I'm thirty-five years old.

*(**NUMBER 7** sits forward.)*

NUMBER 7. Thirty-nine. I'm a salesman.

NUMBER 2. Violent crime? Me?

NUMBER 7. You know, marmalade.

NUMBER 2. No, never.

*(**NUMBER 6** sits forward.)*

NUMBER 6. Oh, yeah, I'm a house painter.

NUMBER 2. I'm a "people person."

(Sound effect: Clock fading under.)

*(**NUMBER 11** sits forward.)*

NUMBER 11. *(German accent.)* Watchmaker, please.

NUMBER 6. Three boys, one girl.

NUMBER 7. My pop? It's complicated.

NUMBER 2. He passed away several years ago.

(**NUMBER 9** *sits forward.*)

NUMBER 9. Sixty-eight, retired, thank you very much.

(**NUMBER 8** *sits forward.*)

NUMBER 8. A brand new baby boy.

(**NUMBER 12** *sits forward.*)

NUMBER 12. Madison Avenue. Ads, jingles, TV.

(**FOREMAN (NUMBER 1)** *sits forward.*)

FOREMAN. America's the greatest country in the world, bar none.

(**NUMBER 5** *sits forward.*)

NUMBER 5. I live up in Harlem. Yeah, sure.

NUMBER 12. Harvard. Oh, thanks.

NUMBER 11. Germany, near to Leipzig.

FOREMAN. Assistant football coach. Out in Queens.

NUMBER 11. Yes, of course, my father.

NUMBER 9. And one great-grandchild on the way.

NUMBER 6. I was jumped once, does that count?

NUMBER 5. Sometimes you hear screams.

NUMBER 12. And I hope I never do.

FOREMAN. My father?

NUMBER 12. World's Greatest Dad.

NUMBER 8. I guess he was my hero.

NUMBER 4. An outstanding judge of character.

(Sound effect: Clock tacet.)

NUMBER 9. Taught me everything I know.

NUMBER 2. Who doesn't love their Dad, right?

NUMBER 4. Not since I was five.

NUMBER 3. Made me the man I am.

NUMBER 10. Justice? Sure, I believe in justice, it's the American way, know what I mean?

NUMBER 9.
The Death
Penalty?

   NUMBER 4.
   If the punishment
   fits the crime.   **NUMBER 8.**
          Life and Death,
   FOREMAN.   yes.
   I can handle
   that.   **NUMBER 5.**

NUMBER 10.   I mean, yes.
Death Penalty,
sure.   **NUMBER 2.**
   An open mind? **NUMBER 6.**
NUMBER 7.   Yeah, sure.
Wide open.   **NUMBER 4.**
   Yes, of course I
   can.   **NUMBER 6.**
   FOREMAN. Why not?
   Totally.   **NUMBER 5.**

NUMBER 9.   Sure.
To the best of
my abilities, yes. **NUMBER 3.**
   Absolutely.
           NUMBER 8.
           Yes, I understand.
           Beyond a
           reasonable doubt.

(The **JURORS** *rise as a group; all raise their right hands:)*

[MUSIC NO. 02 – THE OATH]

GROUP 3. *(Three* **JURORS.**)
I DO SOLEMNLY SWEAR...

GROUPS 1 & 2. *(Six* **JURORS.**)
...THAT I WILL WELL AND
TRULY TRY...

TRULY TRY...

GROUP 1.
(Three **JURORS.**) **GROUP 2.**
AND A TRUE *(Three* **JURORS.**)
DELIVERANCE AND A TRUE **GROUP 3.**
MAKE, DELIVERANCE... ...A TRUE
DELIVERANCE...

ALL.
AND ONE TRUE VERDICT RENDER,
ACCORDING TO THE EVIDENCE...
SO HELP ME...

(We hear the loud clang of a door slamming shut, locking the men in the Jury Room.)

[MUSIC NO. 03 – HOTTEST DAY OF THE YEAR]

(Lights up on a stiflingly hot Jury Room, as the **JURORS** *move their chairs around a long table. There is a wall of dirty windows on one side, looking down and out over the steaming city. Ominous, grey clouds gather over the skyline, full of stormy portent. The grimy windows are all shut in the stuffy room.)*

(A men's room door leads to an offstage lavatory.)

(A display easel holds a diagram of the murdered man's apartment.)

*(The **JURORS** sift around the room in shifting clumps, slowly staking the parameters of their space; ties loosen, jackets hang on sweaty bodies. They get cups of water from the cooler, roll up their sleeves, place their hats on racks, etc.)*

*(**NUMBER 4** reads a newspaper in his chair. Not a bead of sweat on him.)*

*(Several **JURORS** try to open the windows.)*

NUMBERS 2, 4 & 8.
ANOTHER HEAT WAVE...

NUMBERS 6, 9 & 11.
ANOTHER SCORCHER.

FOREMAN, NUMBERS 5 & 12.
MUST BE ONE HUNDRED AND TEN DEGREES.

NUMBERS 4, 7 & 10.
WHAT A TRIAL!

NUMBERS 2 & 5.
WHAT A CIRCUS.

NUMBER 3.
I'LL PROB'LY CATCH A FEW MORE Z'S.

*(To **NUMBER 2**.)* Ya hear me snoring in there?

NUMBER 2. I don't know, it was pretty interesting.

NUMBER 3. Lot of yappin' over nothing.

NUMBER 6.
I'M LOSING WORK...

NUMBER 3.
THREE WHOLE DAYS OF TORTURE!

FOREMAN.
THIS AIN'T EXACTLY MY EXPERTISE.

NUMBER 2.

FASCINATING CASE...

NUMBER 5.

I HATE THIS PLACE...

(**NUMBER 7** *tries the wall fan; it does not work.*)

NUMBER 7.

OH, GREAT.

The fan's busted.

NUMBER 11.

I'M VOTING "GUILTY" WITH NO MISGIVING.

NUMBER 4.

THIS TENDS TO HAPPEN WITH KIDS LIKE THESE.

NUMBER 7.

OPEN-SHUT...

NUMBER 12.

I'M DECIDED. BUT...

NUMBER 10.

HOLY CRAP; WHO CUT THE CHEESE?!

ALL.

IT'S THE HOTTEST DAY OF THE YEAR!

NUMBER 9.

THIS WEATHER WON'T QUIT.

NUMBER 4.

BOY, THE CITY'S A PIT.

ALL.

IT'S THE HOTTEST DAY OF THE YEAR.

FOREMAN.

...AND WE GOT A WAYS TO GO...

(**NUMBER 5** *tries the door handle; discovers it is locked.*)

NUMBER 10. What's the matter with you?

NUMBER 5. I never knew they locked the door.

NUMBER 10. Sure they lock it, just like the clink, know what I mean?

(**NUMBER 5** *approaches his chair, to find* **NUMBER 6** *sitting in it.*)

NUMBER 5. (*To* **NUMBER 6.**) I think that's my chair.

(**NUMBER 4** *takes charge with authority.*)

NUMBER 4. (*To* **NUMBER 6.**) We're sitting in order.

(**NUMBER 6** *immediately rises, offering the seat.*)

NUMBER 6. Oh, sorry.

NUMBER 5. (*To* **NUMBER 4.**) Thanks.

(**NUMBER 5** *takes it, as* **NUMBER 6** *moves away.*)

NUMBER 6.
I'LL DO MY DUTY, BUT THERE'S BILLS TO PAY.

NUMBER 11.
THIS IS THE AMERICAN WAY...

NUMBER 7.
WILL WE BE HERE ALL DAY?

NUMBER 3.
THEY GOT US IN A STRANGLEHOLD.

NUMBER 10.
DAMN THIS SUMMER COLD...

NUMBER 9.

MAN, I'M GETTING TOO OLD FOR THIS.

NUMBER 5. *(Looking around the room.)*

AND ONCE AGAIN, LOOKS LIKE I'M THE ONLY ONE.

NUMBER 2.

ONE HAS TO HELP THE SYSTEM RUN...

NUMBER 12.

GUESS THEY DON'T CALL IT "CIVIC FUN."

NUMBER 6.

I WONDER, IS IT
SAFE TO SPEAK
MY MIND HERE?

NUMBER 2.

FASCINATING!

NUMBER 6.

I'LL DO MY DUTY.

NUMBER 4.

THIS TENDS TO
HAPPEN...

NUMBER 12.

I'M DECIDED...

NUMBER 5.

AND ONCE
AGAIN...

NUMBER 12.

BUT...

NUMBER 3.

THREE WHOLE
DAYS...

THREE WHOLE
DAYS...

THREE WHOLE
DAYS...!

NUMBER 10.

DAMN THIS
SUMMER...

NUMBER 9.

I WONDER WHAT
I'VE SIGNED UP
FOR...

FOREMAN.

EXPERTISE.

NUMBER 11.

THE AMERICAN
WAY.

NUMBER 7.

GOD, GET ME OUTTA HERE...!

ALL.

IT'S TOUGH ENOUGH JUST TO MAKE A LIVING...
WHEN THINGS LIKE JUSTICE DON'T INTERFERE!

NUMBERS 4 & 7.
LET'S MAKE THIS BRIEF,

NUMBERS 4, 7, 11 & 12.
AND FIND RELIEF,

NUMBERS 2, 4, 7, 8, 11 & 12.
OR ELSE WE'RE STUCK,
AND

ALL.
JUST MY LUCK!
IT'S THE HOTTEST DAY OF THE YEAR!

NUMBERS 4, 5, 9 & 10.
CHOKE ON THE DIRT,

NUMBERS 3, 4, 5, 6, 9 & 10.
WHILE YOU SOAK
THROUGH YOUR SHIRT!

ALL.
IF YOU THINK I'M GLAD TO BE HERE,
THEN BUDDY, THE HELL YOU KNOW!

WITH TEMP'RATURES ON THE RISE,
THE PRESSURE INTENSIFIES!

BETTER WATCH OUT,
'CAUSE SOMETHING'S ABOUT

TO BLOW...!!

> (*The* **MEN** *take their seats. The* **FOREMAN**
> *stands.*)

FOREMAN. (*Immediately after music stops.*) Gentlemen, I guess I just want to say that, well, you know, murder in the first degree is just about as serious as it gets.

NUMBER 4. (*Cutting in.*) However we decide, our verdict must be unanimous.

FOREMAN. Right. Like the judge said, unless we find, you know, a reasonable doubt, the death sentence is mandatory, in this case, the electric chair.

NUMBER 3. *(To* **FOREMAN.***)* We know that.

NUMBER 7. Yeah, come on, already, let's go, Modjelewski's pitching tonight, kid's got an arm on him you wouldn't believe –

FOREMAN. Anybody doesn't want to vote? No? Alright, okay then, I mean, I guess we can go ahead and take a vote. This has to be a twelve-to-nothing vote either way. That's the law. Okay, are we ready? All those voting "guilty" raise your hands.

> *(***NUMBERS 3**, **4** *and* **10** *raise their hands immediately. The others go up more slowly.* **NUMBER 9**'s *hand goes up last, and all hands are now raised except for* **NUMBER 8**.)*

Nine-ten-eleven. That's eleven for "guilty."

Okay. "Not guilty"?

> *(***NUMBER 8** *slowly raises his hand.)*

NUMBER 10. *(Under his breath.)* Figures.

FOREMAN. One. Right. Okay.

Eleven to one – guilty as charged.

And now we know where we stand.

NUMBER 10. Boy oh boy, there's always one.

NUMBER 2. One what?

> *(***NUMBER 10** *blows his nose, loud.)*

NUMBER 7. *(To* **NUMBER 10**.*)* Well, your horn works, now try your lights.

NUMBER 10. *(Coughing.)* Something's going around and I got it, damn summer cold.

NUMBER 2. Oh, they're the worst. Would you care for a cough drop, friend? Smith Brothers. *Mentholated.*

NUMBER 10. *(Over-polite.)* Well, don't mind if I do, friend.

(NUMBER 2 *gives* **NUMBER 10** *a cough drop.)*

NUMBER 4. *(To* **NUMBER 8.**) I'm curious as to what you're unsure of. It's rather a cut and dried case.

NUMBER 3. *(To* **NUMBER 8.**) You really think he's innocent?

NUMBER 8. I don't know.

NUMBER 3. I mean, let's be reasonable, you saw the evidence, you could tell the kid was a natural born killer.

NUMBER 8. I don't know about that.

NUMBER 10. Whattya mean you don't know?

NUMBER 2. I guess he means he's not sure if the boy is guilty or not.

NUMBER 10. I know what he means.

NUMBER 5. Then why did you ask?

NUMBER 3. *(To* **NUMBER 8.**) No, I don't get it, you sat in court just like us.

NUMBER 7. You heard what he did.

NUMBER 3. I mean, whattya want?

NUMBER 8. I want us to talk.

[MUSIC NO. 03A – UNDERSCORE]

NUMBER 3. About what?

NUMBER 8. About the evidence –

NUMBER 10. Who the hell are you, Perry Mason?

NUMBER 2. I love Raymond Burr.

NUMBER 3. We heard the evidence!

NUMBER 10. They talked for three whole days, back and forth!

NUMBER 12. I thought the prosecuting attorney was really sharp, the way he hammered home his points, one by one, in logical sequence.

NUMBER 7. Come on, I don't wanna miss the game!

NUMBER 3. Look, the man's a killer, that's a proven fact.

NUMBER 9. He's a boy of sixteen.

NUMBER 5. He's a kid.

NUMBER 3. He's old enough to take a knife and drive it four inches into his father's chest.

NUMBER 10. It's those people! I'm telling you they let the kids run wild up there.

NUMBER 4. He's simply a product of his environment.

NUMBER 6. For what it's worth, I was convinced from the very first day.

NUMBER 12. Ditto. Kid is guilty with a capital G.

NUMBER 7. Open and shut case.

NUMBER 6. Even had like a motive, right?

NUMBER 3. Look, eleven men at this table agree, so what the hell do you want?

NUMBER 9. *(In* **NUMBER 8***'s defense.)* I believe the man wants to talk.

NUMBER 10. *(Loud.)* About what, for Chrissakes? Kid's no damn good, like all the rest of 'em, know what I mean?

NUMBER 2. Well, according to the Prosecutor –

NUMBER 10. *(Interrupting.)* There, you see? Thanks, friend.

NUMBER 2. I didn't finish my sentence, friend.

NUMBER 3. *(To **NUMBER 8.**)* You don't believe the kid is innocent, do you?

NUMBER 8. Maybe I don't.

[MUSIC NO. 04 – THE VERY LEAST]

NUMBER 3. Maybe you don't?

NUMBER 7. So, what'd you vote "not guilty" for?

NUMBER 8.
IT'S NOT EASY TO RAISE MY HAND AND SEND A BOY OFF
    TO DIE.
THAT KIND OF POWER –
AND YET, WE HARDLY KNOW HIM...

KICKED AROUND SINCE HE WAS SMALL,
HIS MOM DECEASED
WHEN HE WAS TWO,
HIS DAD'S A THIEF,
A DRUNK. IT'S TRUE,
THAT'S NOTHING NEW...
I'M JUST ASKING YOU,

ISN'T AN HOUR
THE VERY LEAST
WE OWE HIM?

THAT'S ALL I'M SAYING:

ISN'T AN HOUR THE VERY LEAST WE OWE HIM?

NUMBER 10. *(Interrupting him.)* We don't owe him nothing, am I right?

NUMBER 9. Personally, I'm more than willing to put in an hour.

NUMBER 2. Me, too. This is my first time on a jury. I want the full experience.

NUMBER 10. Listen, those people are just no damned good, liars and thieves and murderers each and every blessed one of them.

NUMBER 6. That's a pretty broad thing to say, buddy, you don't really mean it.

NUMBER 10. What, it's the truth, my friend. Look, I run three garages around town, I seen all kinds. I'm a people expert, I call a spade a spade, know what I mean?

(Aside, to **NUMBER 9.***)* No offense.

(**NUMBER 9** *looks at* **NUMBER 10.***)*

(**NUMBER 7** *laughs.* **NUMBER 3** *and* **NUMBER 12** *laugh, socially.* **NUMBER 2** *laughs, but is not sure why. Others suffer the awkward moment.)*

NUMBER 7. Ha ha none taken.

NUMBER 9. Speak for yourself, son.

NUMBER 10. What, I'm kidding, it's a joke.

NUMBER 9. *(To* **NUMBER 10.***)* It suddenly occurs to me that this man needs to learn a thing or two.

NUMBER 10. *(About* **NUMBER 9.***)* Hey, now what's he goin' on about?

NUMBER 9. Do you think you have a monopoly on the truth? Well, you don't!

NUMBER 3. Alright, it's not Sunday, we don't need a sermon.

NUMBER 10. Monopoly! Oh, come off it now, Grandpa!

FOREMAN & NUMBER 6. Hey –

(**NUMBER 12** *looks up from his doodling.)*

NUMBER 12. Well, it seems to me it's up to us to convince this gentleman that we're right and he's wrong. So, maybe if we each took a minute or two, you know, once around the table. I mean, it's just a quick thought, I figure let's run it up the flagpole and see who salutes it.

NUMBER 11. Flagpole?

FOREMAN. No, good, I like that, let's do it.

NUMBER 7. *(To* **FOREMAN.***)* Alright Mr. Foreman, once around the table,

[MUSIC NO. 05 – ONCE AROUND THE TABLE]

start us off, the clock is ticking, come on –

FOREMAN. Okay. Number One? Oh, that's me. Well…

MAYBE HE'S A KID.
I STILL BELIEVE HE DID IT.
GUILTY. HOW ABOUT YOU?

NUMBER 2.

WELL… I…

NUMBER 3. Listen, here's what I think…

NUMBER 2. Wait a minute…

NUMBER 3.

WHY?

I'M PRESSIN' ON. WITHOUT YOU.

NOW.

THE OLD MAN DOWNSTAIRS,
HE HEARD THE BOY YELL,
"I'LL KILL YOU! I'LL KILL YOU!
SEE YOU IN HELL!"

THE NEXT THING YA KNOW,
HE HEARS *SOMETHING* FALL.

NUMBER 3.
> HE GETS TO HIS DOOR;
> SEES THE KID RUN DOWN THE HALL!
>
> THAT'S SERIOUS, MY FRIEND.
> PERIOD, THE END.
> THAT'S ALL.

NUMBER 4. *(Removing his glasses, cleaning them.)* The boy's entire story was flimsy. He claimed he was at the movies during the time of the killing and yet one hour later, he couldn't remember what films he saw.

NUMBER 3. That's right!

NUMBER 10.
> AND DIDN'T THE OLD BAG
>   ACROSS THE TRACKS

FOREMAN.
> Fellas…

> GET A GOOD GANDER AT THE
>   MANIACS?
> *(Shouted in rhythm.)* YEAH!

ALL OTHERS.

> SHE WATCHED FROM HER BED: OOH…
> THE KID WAS POSSESSED!
> SLAMMIN' A SWITCHBLADE –   (YEAH…)
> *BAM!* IN POP'S CHEST!   *BAM!*

NUMBER 8.
> YES.

She saw the boy through the windows of a passing el train.

NUMBER 10.
> …WHICH THEY PROVED IN COURT
> YOU CAN SEE RIGHT THROUGH,
> SO TOUGH LUCK, SPORT,
> AND NUTS TO YOU!

NUMBER 8.
> SO YOU TAKE HER WORD,
> BUT NOT HIS.

NUMBER 10.
> I DO!
> SO WHAT?!

NUMBER 8.
> GOT ME THERE.
> GLAD WE TALKED IT THROUGH.

NUMBER 10.
> WELL, AIN'T YOU SMART!

NUMBER 6.
> COME ON. DON'T START.

NUMBER 3. Okay, sit down, keep your shirt on.

NUMBER 10. *(Sotto.)*
> WELL, WHO IN THE HELL DOES HE THINK HE IS?!

NUMBER 11. Pardon, gentlemen.

NUMBER 10.
> I'M SICK OF THAT HIGH-AND-MIGHTY TONE OF HIS.

NUMBER 7. What are you letting him get you all upset for?

FOREMAN. Okay, enough already. We have a job to do. Come on, who's next?

NUMBER 5. Can I pass?

FOREMAN. I guess that's your right.

(To **NUMBER 6.***)* You're up. Help me out…?

NUMBER 6. All you need's a motive, right? Didn't the neighbors say something about an argument?
> AND THEN THEY HEARD HIM LEAVE
> 'ROUND SEVEN IN THE EVENING,
> AFTER HE GOT SLAPPED.

NUMBER 11. No...

NUMBER 8. All true, but nothing out of the ordinary.

NUMBER 4.
WELL, *SOME*THING MUST'VE SNAPPED!

NUMBER 11.
NOT SEVEN...

NUMBER 7.
WAIT.

NUMBER 11.
...EIGHT.

NUMBER 7.
THE KID'S OH-FOR-FOUR:
IN JUVIE AT TEN,
REFORM SCHOOL BY FOURTEEN –
AND NOW LOCKED UP AGAIN!

STRIKE THREE. HE'S SHOT HIS WAD.
ANOTHER CHANCE?
YEAH.
GOD FORBID.

NUMBER 8. His father beat him with his fists, every day, since the boy was six.

NUMBER 7. Kid like that? Hell, so would I.

NUMBER 3. Maybe he was teaching him how to survive.

NUMBER 6. Don't that sound like a motive for killing your old man?

NUMBER 8.
SOUNDS MORE LIKE A MOTIVE TO GROW UP AN ANGRY KID.

NUMBER 3. Angry? Hostile! Kids these days show no goddamn respect, am I right?

NUMBER 7. And how!

NUMBER 3. When I was a boy, I called my old man "sir" –

NUMBER 8. Dads don't seem to care much about that kind of thing anymore.

NUMBER 3. Oh yeah? What do you know?

NUMBER 8. I have a six-month-old son of my own at home.

NUMBER 3. Six months, huh?

NUMBER 6. I got four kids, seven, five, four and two.

FOREMAN. Three boys, eleven to three.

NUMBER 4. I have two girls. They can be quite a handful.

NUMBER 7. Wait 'til they discover boys.

NUMBER 10. Or vice versa, know what I mean?

>   (**NUMBER 10** *exits to the men's room, making sure to catch the* **FOREMAN**'s *eye.*)

NUMBER 4. Excuse me?

NUMBER 12. He's kidding, don't mind him.

FOREMAN. (*To* **NUMBER 10**.) Make it quick, will ya? We're trying to get someplace.

NUMBER 2. My boy's at home with the mumps. The wife says he looks like Khrushchev.

NUMBER 8. My whole life changed the day he was born.

NUMBER 6. Right?

NUMBER 3. Yeah, just wait. They grow up.

[MUSIC NO. 06 – ASK ME IF I CARE]

KIDS ARE ALL THE SAME:
THEY DON'T WANNA LISTEN.
KNOW-IT-ALLS AND ROUGHNECKS, CHRIST, I SWEAR.

GIVE 'EM ALL YA GOT;
YOU CAN TAKE A NOSEDIVE OFF A CLIFF!
ASK 'EM IF
THEY CARE.

NUMBER 3.

WHEN MY BOY WAS EIGHT,
I CAUGHT HIM RUNNING FROM A FIGHT.
I SAID, "NO SON OF MINE'S A COWARD
AND THE TRAINING STARTS TONIGHT.

SO PUT 'EM UP – I'LL MAKE A MAN OF YOU,
OR KILL YA WHILE I'M TRYING TO!"

AND THEN, BEFORE I KNEW...

HE GOES AND TURNS FIFTEEN,
BIG AND DUMB AND USELESS –
BAM! HE KNOCKS MY TOOTH OUT... THAT ONE? THERE.

DOESN'T COME AROUND
TWO NOW, MAYBE THREE YEARS. WHAT'S THE DIFF?
ASK ME IF
I CARE.

(An awkward silence, a throat clears.)

[MUSIC NO. 07 – NEVER TOO EASY]

FOREMAN. *(To* **NUMBER 3** *and the others.)* Toughest job there is, am I right?

NUMBER 7. Come on already, the game starts in an hour.

FOREMAN.

BEING A FATHER IS FAR FROM A SURE THING.
IT'S NEVER TOO EASY AT ALL.

NUMBER 3. Gee, thanks Coach.

FOREMAN.

THEY RUN AND THEY WIN AND THEY CLIMB AND THEY
    FALL.

YOU NEED THEM TO KNOW HOW TO CHOOSE THE
    MATURE THING:
GET BACK UP AND BRUSH OFF THEIR KNEES.

NUMBER 2.
YOU TELL 'EM, "BE A BIG MAN…"

NUMBER 8.
"JUST DON'T STOP CLIMBING TREES…"

FOREMAN.
SEE, IT'S NEVER EASY AT ALL.

NUMBER 7. Yak yak yak.

> (**NUMBER 7** *covers his face with his hat, sits this one out.*)

NUMBER 4.
HANG ON…
LET GO…
TEACH MORE
THAN YOU KNOW.

NUMBER 9.
THROUGH HIS EVERY ENDEAVOR,
REMEMBER, WHATEVER YOU DO…

NUMBERS 2, 8, 9 & 12.
HE'S WATCHING YOU,
POP!

NUMBER 5.
IT'S TRUE.
MY FATHER TAUGHT ME:
"GET RIGHT,
BE POLITE,
BRING HONOR TO YOUR FAM'LY."

NUMBER 12.
"…YOUR COUNTRY!"

NUMBER 2.
"GO GET 'EM, TIGER!"

NUMBER 6.
"WORK HARD."

NUMBER 11.

"STAND FOR SOMETHING."

FOREMAN.

"SHOW SOME RESPECT."

NUMBER 4.

"THE DEVIL'S IN THE DETAILS."

NUMBER 12.

"EXPECT WHAT'S COMIN' TO YA –"

NUMBER 3.

"TRY NOT TO BE A JERK."

NUMBER 11.

YEARS GO...

BEFORE YOU
KNOW.

NUMBER 4.

SO SLOW...

BEFORE YOU
KNOW.

**FOREMAN,
NUMBERS 2, 6 & 8.**

THEN, BEFORE
YOU KNOW...

NUMBER 3.

BLINKING BACK AT YOUR SON,
YOU COULD FIND YOURSELF
WONDERING WHO

NUMBERS 4, 5, 9 & 12.

WHO...

HE GREW INTO...

FOREMAN.

BUT, AFTER ALL,
YOU'RE RAISING A MAN,
NOT A WEAK, INSECURE THING.
SO HELP KEEP HIS EYE

FOREMAN, NUMBERS 4, 6 & 12.

ON THE BALL!

NUMBER 9.

AND HOPE FOR THE BEST, WHILE HE LEARNS BY
DEGREES...

NUMBER 2.

FROM *CAT IN THE HAT* TO THE BIRDS AND THE BEES.

NUMBER 8.
> ALTHOUGH, EVEN SO,
> THERE ARE NO GUARANTEES…

FOREMAN.
> …AND THAT'S NEVER EASY AT ALL.

NUMBER 3. *(To* **NUMBER 8.***)* Talk to me in fifteen years. I gotta take a leak.

> (**NUMBER 3** *exits to the men's room.*)

> (**NUMBER 11** *looks at* **NUMBER 12,** *doodling on his paper.*)

NUMBER 11. I beg pardon, what are you doing?

NUMBER 12. Just doodling, a habit of mine.

NUMBER 11. "Rice Pops"?

NUMBER 12. "The breakfast with the built in bounce." One of my clients, I wrote that line, thanks.

FOREMAN. Gentlemen –

NUMBER 11. It's very catchy.

> (**NUMBER 10** *re-enters from the men's room.*)

FOREMAN. We're trying to get someplace.

> *(To* **NUMBER 10.***)* Come on, pal, take your seat, thanks. Now, who's up?

NUMBER 4. Mr. Foreman, we should probably wait until we are all present.

FOREMAN. Oh, uhm, right – you're right.

NUMBER 12. Well, you know, while we're waiting, they have all these statistics about these kinds of kids.

NUMBER 10. Ya see, they got statistics!

NUMBER 4. And the statistics don't paint a pretty picture, I'm afraid.

NUMBER 5. *(Emphatically.)* But statistics can only tell you so much!

(**NUMBER 3** *re-enters from the men's room.*)

FOREMAN. *(Seeing* **NUMBER 3.***)* Okay, great, now that we're all back, you know, I was just thinking, what about all that business with the psychiatrist?

NUMBER 10. I wouldn't give you a wooden nickel for that psycho crap.

FOREMAN. Do you mind, pal? I'm trying to make a point here.

NUMBER 10. Listen, I've got three pinko-shrinkos keeping their cars in one of my garages. Heads up their asses with their diplomas and degrees, know what I mean?

FOREMAN. What I was gonna say was, like with the inkblots and the stuff about his mother, the psychiatrist said the kid is definitely the type that might have killer tendencies, am I right?

NUMBER 12. You're right. I think he said something about internalized paranoid tendencies.

FOREMAN. Right. *(Unsure.)* Uhm, exactly.

NUMBER 11. I beg pardon, but in discussing –

NUMBER 10. I beg pardon, I beg pardon… What are you so friggin' polite about?

NUMBER 11. *(Pleasantly.)* For the same reason you are not. It's the way I was brought up. *(To the* **JURORS.***)* To say that a man is capable of murder does not mean that he has committed murder. Perhaps we would find that if we twelve men took the same tests, one or two of us might be discovered to have unconscious desires to kill. But it does not mean we would carry them out.

NUMBER 10. Listen, if these whatyoucall experts said the kid is capable of murder, then he's capable of murder!

NUMBER 11. But under the right circumstances, aren't we all? Have we learned nothing from the last twenty-five years?

NUMBER 10. Yeah, the Nips and the Krauts can't be trusted as far as you can spit.

NUMBER 6. *(To* **NUMBER 10**, *about* **NUMBER 11.***)* No, this gentleman's got a point.

NUMBER 5. *(About* **NUMBER 11.***)* He's right.

NUMBER 2. Besides, a minute ago you said you wouldn't give a wooden nickel for that "pinko-shrinko psycho-crap."

NUMBER 10. Thanks, Bright-eyes.

NUMBER 2. *(Slightly miffed.)* Don't mention it.

NUMBER 4. Gentlemen, let's stay on point: due to circumstances beyond anyone's control, the boy was born in a ghetto, in a slum. I'm very sorry for him, but it's a well-documented fact: children from ghetto backgrounds are potential menaces to society.

NUMBER 10. Sure, it's not their fault, they don't know no better, am I right? Like Einstein here said *(Indicating* **NUMBER 11.***)*, it's how they're brought up.

NUMBER 11. Pardon, but I grew up in a ghetto just outside Leipzig.

NUMBER 4. While there are, of course, cultural as well as socio-economic elements that imprison the poor within their limited means, I believe –

NUMBER 10. Oh sure, but the problem is, you can't understand them half the time, yapping away a mile a minute, boozing and flaunting it around –

NUMBER 4. That's not at all what I mean...

NUMBER 6. I'm sorry, what exactly do you mean?

NUMBER 4. Well, I, what I was going to say –

NUMBER 10. *(Interrupting.)* Listen, I'm talkin' about the kind of kid who'd ram a knife into his papi's chest soon as look at him. Like he says, it's part of their culture, know what I mean?

NUMBER 6. You mean cuz he speaks Spanish? Because, hey, I'm Mexican.

NUMBER 10. You don't say.

NUMBER 6. Yeah, I am. I mean I was born here, but yeah.

NUMBER 3. Huh.

NUMBER 7. How about that.

> *(The* **JURORS** *all turn to look at* **NUMBER 6**, *who is not comfortable with the attention.)*

NUMBER 6. I mean, I can't speak for everyone, but I was raised to honor my parents, especially my "papi."

NUMBER 7. Sure, sure, he's not talking about you.

[MUSIC NO. 08A – KNOW WHAT I MEAN (PART 1)]

NUMBER 10. You're one of the good ones, anyone can see that.

NUMBER 2. *(Under his breath.)* Oh, boy –

FOREMAN. *(To* **NUMBER 10**.*)* Come on, pal, give someone else a chance to speak.

NUMBER 10.
> I SAY WHAT EVERYBODY'S THINKIN';
> THEY'RE JUST TOO GUTLESS T' COME CLEAN.
>
> I AIN'T THE TIMID SORT!
> TALK'S CHEAP AND LIFE IS SHORT.
> SO, DRY THEM TEARS, DON'T MAKE A SCENE...
>
> *(Specifically to* **NUMBER 2**.*)* Madam.
>
> SOMETIMES MY WIT TAKES TIME TO SINK IN...

Yeah? ...No?

YOU ONLY GOT TO USE YOUR BEAN...

(Specifically to **NUMBER 6.***)*
AND THAT MEANS BRAINS!

SO, IF YOU GET UPSET,
YOU AIN'T HOID NOTHIN' YET!

WHETHER I'M CONVERSIN',
POKIN' FUN, OR CURSIN',
HEY, IT'S NOTHIN' PERSONAL,
Y'KNOW WHAT I –

NUMBER 5.	*(Cutting off* **NUMBER 10***; to* **FOREMAN.***)*
I thought you were in charge here...?

NUMBER 4. *(Cutting off* **FOREMAN.***)* I suggest we get back
to the business at hand.

NUMBER 10. I'm just telling it like it is, sonny boy; the
whole lot of 'em, friggin' slumrats poking around the
garbage looking for a free handout –

NUMBER 5. *(Cutting him off.)* No, I'm sorry, I nurse those
slumrats in Harlem Hospital six nights a week.

NUMBER 10. Relax, Florence Nightingale, you'll get your turn.

[MUSIC NO. 08B – KNOW WHAT I MEAN (PART 2)]

NUMBER 5. You don't know what you're talking about. I've
lived in a slum all my life. I used to play in a backyard
that was filled with garbage.

NUMBER 10. I'm not talkin' about you.

NUMBER 5. Here, take a whiff, maybe you can still smell
it on me!

NUMBER 10. Don't be so damned touchy!

NUMBER 7. He's joking already, come on.

NUMBER 5. I didn't come here to be insulted.

NUMBER 10. *(To the room.)*
WHEN DID I SAY, "IS THAT YOU STINKIN'?"
GAWD! I GIVE UP!
GOODNIGHT, IRENE... EILEEN... IRENE... EILEEN... IRENE...

THESE UPTIGHT KINDA FOLK
SHOULD LEARN TO TAKE A JOKE.

(To **NUMBER 7.***)*
AND IT'S EVEN WORSE WHEN
MEN GO INTO NURSIN', GET ME?

(To **NUMBER 5.***)*
NOTHING PERSON–!

NUMBER 5. *(Interrupting.)* It *is* something personal!

NUMBER 12. He didn't mean you. Let's not be so sensitive.

NUMBER 11. This sensitivity I understand.

NUMBER 3. Don't get your panties in a twist over nothing –

NUMBER 10. Sure, it's a joke, Charlie Chan.

NUMBER 5. Jokes are funny.

NUMBER 9. He's not funny.

NUMBER 5. And I'm not Chinese. I'm Korean.

NUMBER 10. Oh yeah, whose side you fight on?

(**NUMBER 7** *chuckles.*)

FOREMAN. *(Cutting him off.)* Guys, can we please stop all
this arguing. We're wasting time here. *(To* **NUMBER 8.***)*
It's your turn. Let's go.

NUMBER 8. Well I didn't expect a turn. I thought you
were all supposed to be convincing me. Wasn't that the
idea?

FOREMAN. Check. I forgot that.

NUMBER 10. Well, what's the difference? He's the one who's keeping us here. Let's hear what he's got to say.

FOREMAN. Now just a second. We decided we were going to try and convince this gentleman. Let's stick to what we said.

NUMBER 10. Ah, stop bein' a such a kid, will you?

FOREMAN. A kid? Who the hell are you, my father?

NUMBER 5. I'm sure it's nothing personal.

NUMBER 10. K-I-D kid!

FOREMAN. *(Button pushed.)* What, just because I'm trying to keep this thing organized? Listen, you want to step up?

NUMBER 10. What are you gettin' so hot about? Calm down, willya?

FOREMAN. Don't tell me to calm down! Here! Here's the chair. Ya think it's a snap? Come on. Mr. Foreman, let's see how great you'd run the show.

NUMBER 10. Didja ever see such a thing?

FOREMAN. You think this is funny or something?

NUMBER 12. Take it easy. The whole thing's unimportant.

FOREMAN. Unimportant? You want to try it?

NUMBER 12. No. Listen, you're doing a beautiful job. Nobody wants to change.

NUMBER 7. Yeah, you're doing great. Hang in there and pitch.

FOREMAN. All right. Let's hear from somebody. Anybody. Come on.

    (Pause.)

NUMBER 8. Well, according to the testimony, the boy looks guilty. Maybe he is. I sat there in court for three days listening while the evidence built up. I had questions I kept hoping someone would ask, but no one did, not even the kid's own lawyers. I started to think, nothing is that cut-and-dried, what if one of the witnesses made a mistake?

NUMBER 12. Well, then, what's the point of having witnesses?

NUMBER 8. Couldn't they be wrong?

NUMBER 12. They sat on the stand.

NUMBER 3. You saying they lied?

NUMBER 12. They took an oath.

NUMBER 8. They're only people.

NUMBER 7. This is nuts.

NUMBER 4. What are you trying to say?

NUMBER 8. People make mistakes.

NUMBER 12. Well, yes, of course, but they swore under oath on the stand.

NUMBER 8. Could they be wrong?

NUMBER 12. I... No! I don't think so.

NUMBER 8. Do you know so?

NUMBER 12. Nobody can know a thing like that. This isn't an exact science.

NUMBER 8. That's right. It isn't.

NUMBER 3. What difference does it make, the kid is clearly lying through his teeth.

NUMBER 8. Maybe. Maybe not. He swore an oath to tell the truth, who's to say that he didn't?

(*To* **NUMBER 10**.) Do you think he lied?

NUMBER 10. Now, that's a stupid question. Sure he lied.

NUMBER 8. *(To **NUMBER 4**.)* Do you?

NUMBER 4. You know my answer. Yes, he lied.

NUMBER 8. *(To **NUMBER 5**.)* Do you think he lied?

NUMBER 5. I'm not sure…

NUMBER 3. Now, wait a second. You're not sure about what?

NUMBER 5. I'm not sure, okay?

NUMBER 8. *(To the **FOREMAN**.)* I want to call for a Secret Ballot, you eleven vote, I'll abstain. If there are still eleven votes for "guilty," we'll take a guilty verdict in to the judge right now. I won't stand alone. But if anyone votes "not guilty," we'll stay and talk this thing out.

NUMBER 3. Well, finally, you're behaving like a reasonable man.

NUMBER 12. I'll buy that.

NUMBER 7. Okay, let's do it.

FOREMAN. That sounds fair. Anyone doesn't agree? Okay. So, fill out your ballots and then pass them down to me.

[MUSIC NO. 09 – LIGHTS OUT]

*(The **JURORS** take a moment as they fill out their ballots.)*

*(**NUMBER 8** stands apart while they vote.)*

NUMBER 8.

A BOY IS TREMBLING IN A CELL,
DETERMINED HE'LL BE BRAVE,
DENIED THE CHANCE TO SAY FAREWELL
BESIDE HIS DADDY'S GRAVE.

NUMBER 8.
> A MAN IS DEAD.
> ANOTHER MAY DIE.
>
> THE DAYLIGHT SLANTING THROUGH THE BARS
> IS HARD AND STARK AND BLEAK.
> HE HEARS THE WHISPERS OF THE CARS;
> HE SHRUGS TO BRUSH HIS CHEEK,
>
> AND STARES AHEAD,
> TOO *MACHO* TO CRY...
>
> UNTIL LIGHTS OUT,
> WHEN NO ONE SEES HIM IN HIS DARK DESPAIR,
> LIFE HELD SO MUCH PROMISE NOT SO VERY LONG AGO...
>
> AND NOW, AT THIS YOUNG TENDER AGE,
> HIS FUTURE FADES TO BLACK.
> HE CURLS UP IN HIS CONCRETE CAGE,
> AWARE HE CAN'T GO BACK,
>
> WITH PRAYERS UNSAID:
> NO HOPE OF REPLY...
>
> AND THEN LIGHTS OUT,
> WHEN THOUGHTS AND FEARS RUSH IN FROM
>   EV'RYWHERE.
> DOES HE UNDERSTAND THAT HIS NEXT STOP COULD BE
>   DEATH ROW...?
>
> SO I'LL CHOOSE
> TO PUT MYSELF IN HIS SHOES.
>
> HOW CAN COMPASSION
> BE SUCH AN IRRATIONAL TRAIT?
>
> WILL NO ONE ELSE HERE CONCEDE
> THAT EVIDENCE CAN MISLEAD?
>
> WHAT IF WE'VE BEEN TRICKED
> AND WE RUSH TO CONVICT,
> JUST TO FIND OUT ALL TOO LATE...

OH, WELL: LIGHTS OUT,
AND WE'RE THE ONES WHO GAVE SOME KID THE CHAIR!
ALL WE CAN BE SURE OF IS THERE'S SO MUCH WE DON'T
KNOW.

(The **FOREMAN** *reads the ballots one by one:)*

FOREMAN. "Guilty."

"Guilty."

"Guilty."

"Guilty."

"Guilty."

"Guilty."

"Guilty."

"Guilty."

"Guilty."

"Guilty."

"Not Guilty."

The vote now stands ten to two, in favor of "guilty."

NUMBER 3. What in hell!?

NUMBER 10. Boy, oh boy!

NUMBER 7. And another clown flips his wig!

*(***NUMBER 3** *reels on* **NUMBER 5,** *fairly snarling.)*

NUMBER 3. You come in here, vote "guilty" like everybody
else, 'til the preacher over there rips your heart out
with sob stories about a poor little kid with such a hard
life who just couldn't help plunging that knife into his
father's chest, so you change your vote. You make me
wanna goddamn puke!

NUMBER 5. *(To* **FOREMAN.***)* Now, that is *completely*
inappropriate!

NUMBER 4. *(To* **NUMBER 5.***)* All right, all right –

NUMBER 12. He didn't mean anything.

NUMBER 5. *(To* **NUMBER 12.***)* Don't excuse him!

NUMBER 4. He's very excitable.

NUMBER 2. So is dynamite.

NUMBER 7. *(To* **NUMBER 5.***)* So, pretend I'm interested, what made you change your vote?

NUMBER 9. He didn't change his vote. I did.

NUMBER 7. Why am I not surprised?

NUMBER 10. Boy, oh boy –

NUMBER 9. Would you like me to tell you why?

NUMBER 7. No, I would not like you to tell me why!

NUMBER 6. *(To* **NUMBER 7.***)* Pardon me, the man wants to talk.

NUMBER 9. Thank you. This gentleman doesn't say the boy is not guilty. He says he isn't sure. It's not easy to stand alone against the ridicule of others. He gambled for support. I gave it to him. I respect his motives. The boy on trial is probably guilty. But I want to hear more.

NUMBER 7. Yak yak yak.

NUMBER 6. Hey you –

NUMBER 9. I'm talking here!

NUMBER 6. *(To* **NUMBER 9,** *with respect.)* Excuse me, can I say something please?

NUMBER 9. Go ahead.

NUMBER 6. Thanks. Well, I'd like to ask a question. The boy had a motive for the killing, his dad beating on him and all. So if the boy didn't do it, who did?

NUMBER 8. That's not our concern. We're here to decide beyond a reasonable doubt if the boy killed his father, that's all.

NUMBER 4. Examine each point of the evidence, of the specific details. Every little bit paints a portrait of guilt.

NUMBER 3. The old man hears the kid yell "I'm gonna kill you" just before the lady across the street sees the murder through the windows of a passing el train. Then, exactly fifteen seconds later, the old man sees the kid run out of the building.

NUMBER 4. I don't see how you can argue with facts like that.

NUMBER 3. *(To* **NUMBER 8.***)* Well, what have you got to say about it?

NUMBER 8. I don't know.

NUMBER 3. You don't know.

NUMBER 8. Something doesn't sound right to me.

NUMBER 3. Well, suppose you think about it.

> *(He draws a tic-tac-toe board on a piece of paper.)*

(To **NUMBER 12.***)* Come on, let's play tic-tac-toe while Mr. Wizard here figures out the meaning of life.

> *(They play tic-tac-toe.)*

NUMBER 8. Does anyone know how long it takes an elevated train...

NUMBER 3. I'll start: X.

> **(NUMBER 8** *sees the game, angrily snatches up and crumples the paper.)*

NUMBER 8. This isn't a game!

NUMBER 3. Wait a minute!

FOREMAN. Guys, we're wasting time –

NUMBER 8. A boy's life is at stake!

NUMBER 3. Who the hell do you think you are?

NUMBER 10. Martin Luther King?

NUMBER 12. *(To* **NUMBER 3.***)* All right, he didn't mean anything by it, come on, sit down.

NUMBER 10. You gonna take that from him?

NUMBER 6. Calm down, fella.

NUMBER 2. *(To* **NUMBER 10.***)* You're not helping here.

FOREMAN. Hey, hey, hey guys come on!

NUMBER 3. "This isn't a game"?

FOREMAN. Come on, men, no fighting –

NUMBER 12. He didn't mean anything by it.

NUMBER 3. I've got a good mind to belt him one.

NUMBER 10. Go on, hit him, uppity bastard –

FOREMAN. *(Slamming the table.)* I said calm down, damn it!

(Pause. The **FOREMAN** *collects himself.)*

NUMBER 8. I was going to ask if anyone knew about how long it takes a six-car train to pass any given point. Say eight seconds? Ten? Fifteen?

NUMBER 2. Ten seconds. Approximately.

NUMBER 5. That sounds right to me.

NUMBER 6. Sure.

NUMBER 4. Agreed.

NUMBER 10. Come on, what's the guessing game for?

NUMBER 8. Now, tell me, has anyone here ever lived right next to the el tracks?

NUMBER 6. I'm a house painter, y'know, just finished a three day job over in Canarsie right next to the el line.

NUMBER 8. Noisy?

NUMBER 6. Oh, man! Can't hear yourself think.

NUMBER 8. That's right, you can't hear yourself think.

NUMBER 3. Okay. You can't hear yourself think. Get to the point.

NUMBER 8. Alright now, consider this: Since the woman saw the stabbing through the last two cars, we can assume that the body fell to the floor as the train passed by. Therefore, the el train had been passing by the old man's window for a full ten seconds before the body fell. Which means the old man would have had to hear the boy make his statement while the el was roaring past his nose. Which means it's not possible the man heard what he said he did!

NUMBER 3. That's idiotic! Sure he could have heard it.

NUMBER 8. *(To* **NUMBER 3**.*)* Do you think so?

NUMBER 3. The old man said he heard the boy yell "I'll kill you." That's good enough for me.

NUMBER 8. If he heard anything at all, he still couldn't have identified the voice with the el roaring by.

NUMBER 3. You're talking about a matter of seconds. Nobody can be that accurate.

NUMBER 8. We're talking about a boy's life here, it should be that accurate.

NUMBER 5. I don't think he could have heard it. There's no way.

NUMBER 6. Yeah, you look at it like that, maybe he didn't hear it. I mean, with the noise from the train...

NUMBER 10. Of all the crazy ideas –

[MUSIC NO. 10 – JUST WORDS]

NUMBER 8. – But even supposing he did say it, does that mean he actually meant it?

NUMBER 3. Wait a minute! What the hell are you twistin' around here? The boy yelled out, "I'll kill you." Case closed!

NUMBER 8. My point is, he's a bright boy, so why would he –

NUMBER 10. *(Interrupting.)* Bright? He's a common, ignorant slob. He don't even speak good English.

NUMBER 11. He *doesn't* even speak good English.

NUMBER 8.

THEY'RE JUST WORDS:
"I'LL KILL YOU."
WE'VE ALL SAID THINGS WE NEVER MEANT,
EV'RYONE, TO A MAN.

NUMBER 4.

THEY'RE JUST WORDS
UNTIL YOU
ESTABLISH MURDEROUS INTENT –

NUMBER 8.

WHICH I DON'T THINK YOU CAN.

NUMBER 2.

THIS GUY AT WORK, HE CALLED ME IDIOTIC.
PUT-DOWNS AND CHALLENGES WERE HURLED…

WELL,
I MAY HAVE
SAID SOMETHING
NOT SO POLITE,
BUT THAT'S   **NUMBER 8.**
NO CRIME.   NO, IT'S ONLY AN EXPRESSION,
                                   PEOPLE SAY IT ALL THE TIME.

NUMBER 5.
I'LL KILL YA!
I'LL KILL YA!
IS THAT A PROMISE OR A THREAT?

NUMBER 7.
I'LL KILL YA!

NUMBER 2.
I'LL KILL YA!

NUMBER 9.
I SWEAR TO GOD,
I'LL KILL YOU
YET.
(*Continues.*)

NUMBERS 2 & 7.
I'LL KILL YA!
I'LL KILL YA!
(*Continues.*)

NUMBER 5.
JUST WORDS...

NUMBER 4.
I'M GONNA BREAK
YOUR NECK,
HONEY,
I'LL GIVE YOU
SUCH A CRACK.

HURTFUL
    WORDS...

I HAVE

HEARD SOME

**FOREMAN &
NUMBER 12.**
I'LL KNOCK YOUR
BLOCK OFF!
(*Continues.*)

NUMBER 3.
SO HELP ME, ONE
MORE TIME...

NUMBERS 6 & 11.
I'LL CLEAN YOUR
CLOCK!
(*Continues.*)

YOU'D BETTER
KEEP IN
CHECK,
DARLING,

HATEFUL WORDS.

NUMBER 3.
YOU KIDS ARE
ON THIN ICE.

SO HELP ME, ONE
MORE TIME...

BETTER NOT
SASS ME BACK.
(*Continues.*)

NUMBER 10.
SIC 'EM, BOY!
KILL THE
BASTARD!

COME TO THINK
OF IT,

SOME I MYSELF
HAVE SAID.

          NUMBER 10.   **NUMBER 5.**

NUMBER 3.   SIC 'EM BOY!   STILL, NOBODY

    DON'T MAKE ME   *(Continues.)*   WOUND UP

    TELL YOU   DEAD.

    TWICE.

    (Continues.)

        (**JURORS** *continue in background, whispering,*
        as:)

NUMBER 5.

    IF, AS YOU SAY, THIS

       BOY WAS PLOTTING

       VIOLENCE...   **NUMBER 8.**

    WOULD HE ANNOUNCE   ...WOULD HE ANNOUNCE

       IT TO THE WORLD...?   IT TO THE WORLD...?

ALL (EXCEPT NUMBERS 5 & 8).

    I'LL KILL YA!

    I'LL KILL YA!

NUMBER 8.

    THAT'S NOT TO SAY "I'LL   **NUMBER 5.**

       CUT YOUR THROAT."   MISTER FOREMAN, IF YOU

                             PLEASE, I THINK I'D

                             LIKE TO CHANGE MY

                             VOTE.

    (Outbursts interrupt; music fades under.)

NUMBER 3.

    What?!

       NUMBER 12.

         Wait.

           NUMBER 4.

            But the facts!

              NUMBER 7.

               You're kidding!

> **NUMBER 5.**
> "Not guilty"

> **FOREMAN.**
> Are you sure?

NUMBER 5. I'm sure.

NUMBER 3. No!

FOREMAN. The vote is nine to three, in favor of "guilty."

NUMBER 10. Boy, oh boy!

NUMBER 2. This is exciting!

NUMBER 10. Thrill a minute. Gimme one of them cough drops, friend.

NUMBER 2. *(Reprimanding his manners.)* Thank you, please, friend.

NUMBER 10. Yeah yeah yeah –

> (**NUMBER 2** *slides him a cough drop.*)

NUMBER 7. *(To* **NUMBER 5***.)* Listen, I don't know what you're thinking, but there are facts staring you right in your face. Every one of them says this kid killed his old man.

NUMBER 8. Plenty of innocent men have been put to death because sometimes...

NUMBER 7. *(To* **NUMBER 8***.)* I'm talkin' to him, not to you.

NUMBER 8. Because sometimes the facts that are staring you in the face are wrong.

NUMBER 11. Pardon –

NUMBER 7. Is that clock right?? Come on, already!

NUMBER 11. Pardon me, but I have made some notes here.

NUMBER 10. Notes yet!

NUMBER 11. From what was presented at the trial, the boy looks guilty, but maybe if we go deeper –

NUMBER 7. *(To* **NUMBER 11.***)* Look, pal, here in America, facts are facts, you don't need to go any deeper!

NUMBER 11. But, I ask, if he truly had killed his father, why would he come back three hours later? Wouldn't he be afraid of being caught?

NUMBER 4. The boy knew there were people who could identify the knife as the one he had just bought.

NUMBER 11. But if what you say is true, why did he leave it there in the first place?

NUMBER 4. I think we can assume he ran out in a state of panic after he killed his father.

NUMBER 3. Exactly!

NUMBER 11. And yet he was calm enough to ensure there were no fingerprints on the knife. So, please, where did his panic start and where did it end?

NUMBER 3. Listen, you voted "guilty" didn't you? What side are you on?

NUMBER 11. I don't believe I have to be loyal to one side or the other. I am simply asking questions.

NUMBER 12. Well, this is just off the top of my head, but if I were the boy, and I'd, you know, done the stabbing and everything, I'll bet he figured no one had seen him and that the body probably wasn't even discovered yet.

NUMBER 2. After all, it was the middle of the night. Maybe he thought no one would find the body 'til the next day.

NUMBER 11. Pardon. Thank you. And here is my whole point. The boy must certainly have heard the woman across the street screaming for the police as he ran out of the building. Wouldn't he be afraid someone saw?

NUMBER 4. Remember, he lived in a bad neighborhood where screams were fairly commonplace. It could have been one of dozens of screams.

NUMBER 3. Right! There's your answer!

NUMBER 8. Maybe. Maybe he did stab his father. Maybe he didn't hear the woman's screams. Maybe he did run out in a panic. Maybe he did calm down three hours later and came back to try and get the knife, risking being caught by the police. Maybe all those things are so. But maybe they're not.

NUMBER 11. Maybe they are not, yes.

[MUSIC NO. 11 – COINCIDENCE]

NUMBER 4. In my opinion, every step of the boy's testimony is filled with gaps and flights of fancy, but very little factual evidence.

NUMBER 9. Facts can change, can they not?

NUMBER 4. Facts are facts – nothing more, nothing less.

NUMBER 3. Exactly. Just like the knife sonny boy planted in his father's chest.

NUMBER 8. I'd like to see the knife again actually. Mr. Foreman?

> (The **FOREMAN** rises and crosses to the door, knocks. The unseen guard unlocks it, as the **FOREMAN** whispers to him, requesting the murder weapon.)

NUMBER 4.

THE BOY MOUTHS OFF – HIS FATHER SLUGS HIM ONE...

NUMBER 8.

NO, HE SLAPPED –

NUMBER 4.

...WHATEVER – SLAPPED – THIS WAS ABOUT EIGHT O'CLOCK.

NUMBER 4.
> HE LEAVES THE APARTMENT. THEN JUST FOR FUN,
> HE DECIDES TO DO A BIT OF SHOPPING DOWN THE BLOCK.

NUMBERS 2 & 6.
> OKAY...   **FOREMAN & NUMBER 10.**
>   YEAH, RIGHT...

NUMBER 4.
> HE BUYS A PRESENT FOR A SO-CALLED FRIEND.

NUMBER 7.
> IT'S A SWITCHBLADE!

NUMBER 3.
> IT'S A DOOZY!

NUMBER 4.
> NOTHING LIKE IT IN STOCK
> BUT LOSES IT –

NUMBER 10.
> AIN'T THAT THE LIVING END?!

NUMBER 7.
> SHOULDA KNOWN THE
>   HOLE WAS IN HIS
>   POCKET.   **NUMBER 3.**
NUMBER 8.   WHAT A CROCK!
> YOU'RE

saying it couldn't possibly be so...?

NUMBERS 2, 4 & 6.
> NO!   **FOREMAN & NUMBER 12.**
>   IT'S GOSPEL.

NUMBER 4.   **FOREMAN, NUMBERS 2, 6 & 12.**
> SURE!   SURE!
> IT'S PURE
> COINCIDENCE!   COINCIDENCE!

NUMBER 4. Let's see...

> QUARTER TO NINE,
> HE MET THREE BUDDIES OUT IN FRONT OF A DINER.
> HE LET 'EM SEE THE SWITCHBLADE,
> WHICH MADE A VERY BIG IMPRESSION.
> THEY REMEMBERED HIS INDISCRETION
> WHEN THEY WERE QUESTIONED IN COURT.
> HOME AT TEN,
> THEN BACK OUT AGAIN
> T'CATCH A FLICK –
> A PARTICULARLY RICKETY ALIBI: BIG TROUBLE!
> THREE FIFTEEN,
> MURDER SCENE,
> WITH EVIDENCE ENOUGH TO PROVE HE DID IT,
> SO THEY CUFFED HIM ON THE DOUBLE.

*(The **FOREMAN** brings the knife to the table.)*

FOREMAN, NUMBERS 2 & 6 .

> EXHIBIT "A"!

NUMBER 4.

> HEY!

FOREMAN, NUMBERS 2, 4 & 6.

> THAT'S SOME
>   COINCIDENCE!

NUMBERS 3 & 12.

> HEY!
> WHERE'D THAT COME
>   FROM?
>
> COINCIDENCE!

NUMBER 4. Everyone connected with the case identified the knife. Now are you trying to tell me that it really fell through a hole in the boy's pocket and that someone picked it up off the street, went to the boy's house and stabbed his father with it?

NUMBER 8. No. I'm saying that it's possible that the boy lost the knife and that someone else stabbed his father with a similar knife.

NUMBER 4. Oh, brother!

CLEVER FICTION DISTRACTS
FROM DESPICABLE ACTS,
BUT THE FACTS ARE THE FACTS,
AND NOW THEY'RE FROZEN IN PLACE!
AND UNLESS YOU'RE INSANE,
YOU CAN SEE 'EM AS PLAIN
AS THE NOSE ON YOUR FACE!

NUMBERS 3, 6, 7 & 10.
NOW LET'S CLOSE
UP THIS CASE!

NUMBER 4. Take a look at this knife. I've never seen one like it. Neither had the storekeeper who sold it to the boy. Aren't you asking us to accept a pretty incredible coincidence?

NUMBER 8. I'm not asking anyone to accept it.

NUMBER 4.
THE LOGIC A DESPERATE MAN EMPLOYS
ADDS UP TO GUESSWORK AND SO MUCH NOISE!
'CAUSE WHEN YOU MAKE IT UP AS YOU GO ALONG,
YOU'RE BOUND TO GET A COUPLE DETAILS WRONG.

NUMBER 10.
AMEN!
CLEVER FRICTION ATTRACTS
UNEXPLICABLE ACTS!

NUMBERS 7 & 12.
BUT THE FACTS ARE THE FACTS!

NUMBER 4.
THIS KNIFE IS ONE OF A KIND!

NUMBERS 2, 6 & 12.
YEAH!

NUMBERS 4 & 7.
SO GIVE IT A BREATHER.

NUMBERS 4, 6, 7 & 10.
IT'S OVER, AND EITHER

NUMBERS 2, 4, 6, 7, 10 & 12.
YOU'RE LEGALLY BLIND,
OR YOU'RE

FOREMAN, NUMBERS 2, 3, 4, 6, 7, 10 & 12.
OUT OF YOUR MIND!

NUMBER 4. A duplicate weapon?

FOREMAN, NUMBERS 2, 3, 4, 6, 7, 10 & 12.
PLEASE!

NUMBER 4.
HE'S AS GOOD AS DEAD.

NUMBER 8.
I SAID IT'S POSSIBLE.

NUMBER 4.
IMPROBABLE...

> (**NUMBER 8** *reaches into his pocket and withdraws a knife.*)

NUMBER 8.
YEAH,

> (*Holding it in front of his face and flicking it open.*)

BUT POSSIBLE.

> (*He leans forward and sticks the knife into the table. They are exactly alike.*)

ALL (EXCEPT NUMBER 8).
WOW!

(In a tumble.)

NUMBER 6. Look at it! It's the same knife.

NUMBER 7. What is this?

NUMBER 12. Where'd that come from?

NUMBER 5. The knives are identical!

NUMBER 2. How d'you like that?

NUMBER 3. What are you trying to do?

NUMBER 10. What next, ya gonna pull a rabbit outta yer ass?

NUMBER 4. *(To* **NUMBER 8.***)* Where did you get that knife?

NUMBER 8. After the trial yesterday, I was walking for a couple of hours. The knife comes from a little pawnshop about three blocks from the boy's apartment house. It cost a buck fifty.

NUMBER 3. So, it's the same kind of knife. So, what's that mean? It means nothing.

NUMBER 7. Of all the ridiculous...

NUMBER 3. What about the old man downstairs? He said he saw the boy run out of the building. Now, are you accusing the old man of lying under oath?

NUMBER 9. Well, perhaps not intentionally, of course...

NUMBER 5. It stands to reason...

NUMBER 3. You're crazy! Why should he lie? What's he got to gain?

NUMBER 9. Attention, maybe.

NUMBER 3. You keep coming up with these bright sayings. Why don't you send one into Hallmark? They pay three bucks a pop.

NUMBER 6. *(To* **NUMBER 3.***)* Listen, pal, show a little respect.

(*To* **NUMBER 9**.) Go ahead.

NUMBER 9. Thank you. My point is, he may not be the most reliable witness.

NUMBER 6. Why's that?

NUMBER 9. I looked at him, at the details of the man, for a long time.

[MUSIC NO. 12 – SOMEWHERE BETWEEN NOW AND THEN]

He was a very old man with a jacket torn under the left arm, did you notice? He walked very slowly to the stand. He was dragging his left leg and trying to hide it because he was ashamed. The man suffered a stroke not six months ago.

NUMBER 2. But why do you think the old man's lying?

NUMBER 9. Not lying exactly, but...

(*Several* **JURORS** *barely mask their impatience.*)

GETTING ON IS ISOLATING,
CONTEMPLATING
ABSENT FRIENDS.

NUMBER 7. The clock is ticking!

(*He goes to the water cooler.*)

NUMBER 9.
DAY'S FOR WAITING
'TIL IT ENDS,
THEN NIGHT'S FOR SOLITAIRE.

NUMBER 10. Come on already...

(*He steps away from the table, impatient, joins* **NUMBER 7**.)

NUMBER 9.

> THINK REGRETS AND APPREHENSION:
> MEAGER PENSION,
> CHOICES MADE.
> SCANT ATTENTION EVER PAID –
> WELL, WHO SAID LIFE WAS FAIR?
>
> BUT THERE WAS A TIME WHEN THE WORLD WAS YOUNG,
> WHEN ALL HE HAD WAS NOTHING BUT TIME,
> BELIEVING THAT FORTUNE WOULD FAVOR ALL VALIANT
>   MEN...
>
> ALTHOUGH, I GUESS HE GOT THE MESSAGE
> TIME AND TIME AGAIN
> SOMEWHERE BETWEEN NOW AND THEN.

NUMBER 4. I honestly don't see how this impacts the man's testimony.

NUMBER 5. Let him finish.

NUMBER 9.

> TODAY, HE SPEAKS, BUT PEOPLE HEAR HIM.
> CROWDS DRAW NEAR HIM:
> "WHAT'D HE SAY?"
> STREET TOUGHS FEAR HIM;
> NOW THEY'LL PAY!
> AND THAT'S THE WAY IT GOES...
>
> BUT WEREN'T *THOSE* THE DAYS, WHEN THE WORLD WAS
>   YOUNG?
> HE'D CHARGE FULL-BORE, HE'D STOP ON A DIME.
> THE SMUG SELF-ASSURANCE ONE'S ARROGANT YOUTH
>   WILL ALLOW!
>
> HE RAGED, HE RAILED,
> BUT FINDS HE FAILED
> TO MAKE HIS MARK SOMEHOW,
>
> SOMEWHERE BETWEEN THEN AND...

NOW, FATE GRANTS
ONE FINAL CHANCE
TO STAKE HIS CLAIM,
AND WHO CAN BLAME HIM?
ONE LAST SHOT
TO SAY, "I'VE GOT A VOICE! I'M HERE,"
THEN DISAPPEAR...

AS THE YEARS INTERVENE,
YOU'LL SEE WHAT I MEAN
SOMEWHERE BETWEEN NOW AND THEN...

THAT THERE WAS A TIME WHEN THE WORLD WAS
    YOUNG...

NUMBER 8. I'd like to call for another vote.

NUMBER 10. Did hear the scream, didn't hear the scream. What's the difference? They're just little details. You're forgetting the important stuff.

FOREMAN. There's another vote called for.

NUMBER 3. What are we gonna gain by voting again?

NUMBER 2. It only takes a second.

FOREMAN. Okay, all those in favor of "not guilty" raise their hands

        (**NUMBERS 5, 8, 9** *raise hands.*)

Still the same. One, two, three "not guiltys." Nine "guiltys."

NUMBER 7. I'm telling you, we can yakkity-yak until next Tuesday. Where's it getting us?

NUMBER 11. Pardon. (*Raises hand.*) I vote "not guilty."

NUMBER 10. Oy vey!

NUMBER 3. What are you talking about? Are we all going crazy in here?!

FOREMAN. The vote is eight to four, in favor of "guilty."

NUMBER 3. What's with you bleeding hearts already?

(To **NUMBER 11.***)* Tell me why you changed your vote. Come on, give me reasons. I mean real reasons.

NUMBER 11. I have a reasonable doubt in my mind.

NUMBER 7. What reasonable doubt? What does that mean?

NUMBER 9. *(To* **NUMBER 7.***)* He's not the one on trial here.

NUMBER 7. *(To* **NUMBER 11.***)* Honestly, I don't get it. How can you change your vote? I mean, where's your balls, man?

NUMBER 11. I change my vote because I changed my mind; we are all allowed to change our minds, even you.

> **(NUMBER 3** *grabs the switchblade and holds it up.)*

NUMBER 3. Here, look at this knife. The kid you just decided isn't guilty was seen ramming this knife, this very knife right here, into his own father's heart. Here, take it. Now you hold it in your hand and tell me he didn't do it.

NUMBER 9. That's not the actual knife. Don't you remember?

NUMBER 3. Oh, brilliant! *(Sticks knife into table.)*

NUMBER 5. *(To* **NUMBER 4.***)* Stuffy in here, right?

> **(NUMBER 5** *notices there isn't one drop of sweat on* **NUMBER 4.***)*

Pardon me, don't you sweat?

NUMBER 4. No. In fact, I don't.

NUMBER 7. *(To* **NUMBER 8.***)* So, what're we supposed to believe? That the old man didn't hear the boy shout "I'm going to kill you"? He didn't run to his door and see the kid tearing down the stairs fifteen seconds after the body hit the floor? Oh, right, he's only saying that to make himself feel important because he's old... give me a break.

NUMBER 5. Wait, go back, did the old man say he *ran* to the door?

NUMBER 7. Ran, walked. What's the difference? He got there.

NUMBER 9. It makes a difference to an old man with a bad leg.

NUMBER 7. Yak yak yak.

NUMBER 9. Your father should have taught you to respect your elders, son.

NUMBER 7. Can the lecture, pop.

NUMBER 6. He said he ran to the door. At least, I think he did.

NUMBER 4. He said he *went* from his bedroom to the front door in fifteen seconds. Isn't that enough?

NUMBER 8. Wait a minute. Where was his bedroom again?

> (**NUMBER 6** *brings over the easel with the apartment diagram.* **JURORS** *gather around.*)

NUMBER 10. You mean there's something you don't remember? Wait, let me call the *New York Times*!

NUMBER 3. What are you trying to prove here, what a hero you are?

> (**NUMBER 8** *grabs chairs, and with the help of several* **JURORS**, *recreates the old man's apartment. He puts the chairs roughly in place, checking the diagram, pacing off distance between points.*)

NUMBER 8. The old man says he got to the front door of his apartment in fifteen seconds, in time enough to clearly identify the boy as he ran out of the building.

NUMBER 3. He said twenty.

NUMBER 8. He said fifteen.

NUMBER 3. He said twenty!

NUMBER 11. *(Holding up his notes.)* He said fifteen.

NUMBER 3. What's the difference fifteen, twenty? He's an old man, how can he be sure of anything, for Christ's sake?

NUMBER 2. I think that's the point.

> *(**NUMBER 8** places two chairs as the "bed.")*

NUMBER 12. The man said he saw the boy running out. That's pretty irrefutable testimony. Don't you think? Or not.

NUMBER 8. Now, here's the "bed."

NUMBER 10. What the hell?

NUMBER 8. I want to see if an old man dragging his leg behind him because he had a stroke last year can make it to the front door of his apartment in fifteen seconds, as he testified he did.

> *(**NUMBER 8** picks up another chair and paces to the wall, others watch as he counts off the rest of the distance.)*

NUMBER 3. You're crazy.

NUMBER 9. Seems pretty sane to me.

NUMBER 10. You can't recreate a thing like that.

NUMBER 2. Why not?

NUMBER 11. I'd like to see it.

NUMBER 6. So would I.

NUMBER 5. So would I.

FOREMAN. Me too.

NUMBER 7. Come on already –

NUMBER 10. Goddamn waste of time.

FOREMAN. Hey, watch your language, buddy.

NUMBER 8. ...Thirty-nine, forty, forty-one, forty-two, forty-three feet.

> (**NUMBER 2** *brings a chair to* **NUMBER 8**, *who places it.*)

NUMBER 8. So, that's a total of forty-three feet from his bed to the front door of his apartment, in fifteen seconds. Who's got a watch with a second hand?

NUMBER 2. I have.

NUMBER 8. When you want me to start, point, that'll be the body falling. Time me from there. Remember, fifteen seconds.

> (**NUMBER 8** *lies on the two "bed" chairs.*)

NUMBER 3. I've never seen anything like this in my whole life!

NUMBER 7. Anyone for charades?

NUMBER 8. Okay. I'm ready.

[MUSIC NO. 13 – THE BIG IDEA]

> (*Sound effect: Watch.* **NUMBER 2** *stares at his watch, waits.*)

NUMBER 3. He's making a friggin' mockery of this whole thing!

NUMBER 10. Come on, friend, let's get going.

NUMBER 2. I want to wait until the second hand reaches sixty... And...

> (*They wait;* **NUMBER 2** *points.*)

> (**NUMBER 8** *re-enacts the old man's testimony, as* **OTHER JURORS** *count off the seconds.*)

NUMBERS 2, 5, 7 & 11.
ONE.

         NUMBERS 4, 6, 9 & 12.
         ONE THOUSAND,

TWO.

         ONE THOUSAND,

THREE.

         ONE THOUSAND,

FOUR.

         ONE THOUSAND,

FIVE.

         ONE THOUSAND,

SIX.

         ONE THOUSAND,

SEVEN.

         ONE THOUSAND,

EIGHT.

         ONE THOUSAND,

NINE.

         ONE THOUSAND,

TEN.

         ONE THOUSAND,

ELEVEN.

         ONE THOUSAND,

TWELVE.

         ONE THOUSAND,

THIRTEEN.

                  NUMBERS 2 & 11.
         ONE THOUSAND,   *(Split off.)*
FOURTEEN.   TIME'S

         ONE THOUSAND.

                  UP.

NUMBER 10. *(Sotto.)*
OF ALL THE SCHEMES...

NUMBER 3. *(Sotto.)*
THE DIRTY CHEAT...

NUMBER 8.

> OUR WORK, IT SEEMS...
> IS NOT COMPLETE.
> CONSIDER:
> THE OLD MAN HEARS A QUARREL, HOURS BEFORE.
> HE GOES TO BED.
> THEN SOMETHING HITS THE FLOOR.
> A WOMAN SCREAMS
> ACROSS THE STREET.
>
> HE GETS BACK UP,
> AND TRIES TO REACH THE DOOR...
> THEN FOOTSTEPS POUNDING DOWN THE STAIRS.
> HOW DOES HE KNOW IT'S OUR BOY?
> HE SWEARS HE DOES,
> AND THAT'S BECAUSE
> HE *THOUGHT* IT WAS.

NUMBER 6.

> AH, YES, I SEE

NUMBER 7.

> COME ON.

NUMBER 10.

> THAT'S NUTS!

NUMBER 2.

> MAKES SENSE TO ME.

NUMBER 3.

> HAVE YOU ALL GONE BATS?!
> WHAT'S THE BIG IDEA, FELLA?
> HAVE YOU NO GODDAMN SHAME?
> THESE KIDS ARE ALL THE SAME,
> AND OUR SOCIETY'S TO BLAME!
>
> WE GET 'EM OFF; WE SET THEM FREE,
> THEN STEP ASIDE, AND LET THEM BE!

NUMBER 11.
TEMPER, TEMPER.

NUMBER 7.
LET'S GO...
COME ON...

NUMBER 3.
WELL NOT ME,

NUMBER 4.
TAKE IT EASY,
PALLY...

NUMBER 2.
THIS IS SO
EXCITING...!

NUMBER 12.
JUST A
ROADBLOCK.

PAL!

NUMBERS 4 & 11.
NOT THE GRAND
FINALE.

LOOK!

I'm sure things are tough in the ghetto, but that don't mean you get to come in here and make up some sob story. Meanwhile...

...WE'RE LETTIN' HIM GET AWAY...!
HE'S GUILTY, YOU KNOW IT, AND
SO DO I!
LET'S WRAP THIS THING UP, AND
LET ME BUY YOU A BEER.

NOW, GROW SOME BALLS AND ACT
LIKE MEN,
...OR HE'S GONNA SLIP RIGHT
THROUGH OUR FINGERS HERE!
WE ARE

NUMBERS 2, 5, 7 & 12.
OOH...

NUMBERS 3 & 10.
LETTIN' HIM

NUMBERS 3, 4 & 10.
GET

NUMBERS 3, 4, 7 & 10.
AWAY...!

NUMBER 8.

SLIP RIGHT THROUGH
   YOUR FINGERS?
WHAT ARE YOU, HIS
   EXECUTIONER?
EVER SINCE WE GOT HERE,
YOU'VE BEEN GUNNING
   FOR HIM.

NUMBER 3.

GO ON, BE A HERO,
   BUT YOU OFFER NO
   SOLUTION, SIR.
THERE'S NO SECOND
   SHOT HERE,

NUMBER 8.

JUST ASK YOUR SON.

NUMBER 3.

WHAT WAS THAT CRACK?!

NUMBER 8.

FORGET IT.

NUMBER 3.

YOU TAKE THAT BACK!

NUMBER 8.

JUST LET IT BE.

I PITY YOU.

NUMBER 3.

WHO ASKED YOU TO?!

NUMBER 8.

YOU MAKE ME SICK!

NUMBER 3.

SO SUCK MY DICK!

NUMBER 3.

I MIGHT BE ONE...!

NUMBERS 7, 10 & 12.

WHEN WILL WE BE
   DONE...?

NUMBER 5.

THINK THEY'RE GONNA
   FIGHT?

NUMBER 2.

THAT WOULD NOT BE
   RIGHT.

NUMBER 10.

DON'T BE SO UPTIGHT.

NUMBER 7.

WE'LL BE HERE ALL NIGHT.

FOREMAN.

BOYS, IT'S NEVER TOO EASY

FOREMAN & NUMBER 9.

AT ALL...

<table>
<tr><td>NUMBER 8.
  TEMPER, TEMPER.</td><td>FM, #4, 7 & 10.
  HE'S GUILTY!</td><td>NUMBER 6.
  HE'S GUILTY!</td></tr>
<tr><td>NUMBER 3.
  OH, CUT THE CRAP!</td><td>#5, 9 & 11.
  NOT GUILTY!</td><td> NOT GUILTY!</td></tr>
<tr><td>NUMBER 8.
  TEMPER, TEMPER.</td><td>FM, #4, 7 & 10.
  SO GUILTY!</td><td>#2, 6 & 12.
  SO GUILTY!</td></tr>
<tr><td>NUMBER 3.
  AND SHUT YOUR
    TRAP!</td><td>#5, 9 & 11.
  NOT GUILTY!</td><td> NOT GUILTY!</td></tr>
<tr><td>NUMBER 8.
  WOULDN'T YOU LOVE TO
    PULL THAT SWITCH?</td><td colspan="2">OTHERS.
  THIS CASE IS
  A KILLER,</td></tr>
<tr><td>NUMBER 3.
  SON OF A
    MOTHERFUCKING
    BITCH!
  (Overlapping.)
  LET ME GO!!
  I'LL KILL HIM!
  I'LL KILL HIM!
  I'LL KILL HIM!</td><td colspan="2"> A KILLER.
  A KILLER,
  (Overlapping.)
  A KILLER,
  A KILLER,
  A KILLER,
  A KILLER.</td></tr>
</table>

NUMBER 8. Now you don't really mean you'll kill me, do you?

(All eyes are on **NUMBER 3** *and* **NUMBER 8,** *standing toe to toe.)*

NUMBER 2. Mr. Foreman, I'd like to change my vote to "not guilty."

NUMBER 6. Yeah, me too – "not guilty."

NUMBER 7. You gotta be kidding me.

FOREMAN. Anyone else?

(No one speaks.)

Uhm, okay, the score, I mean the count now stands at six to six.

NUMBER 3. Unbelievable!

(**NUMBER 3** *storms off to the men's room, slamming the door behind him.*)

(*Almost in response, the skies open up, and a downpour of rain drops on the city.*)

(*Sound effect: rainfall.*)

(*The* **JURORS** *adjust the windows as the rain pelts the glass.*)

NUMBER 6. Wow! Look at that come down, willya?

NUMBER 2. Think it'll cool things off?

NUMBER 6. Yeah I guess so.

NUMBER 2. Thank goodness.

(*The* **FOREMAN** *turns on the overhead lights.*)

FOREMAN. I guess let's take a quick five here. If anybody needs to hit the head, now's a good time –

(**NUMBER 7** *manages to turn on the fan.*)

NUMBER 7. Hey, hey, whattya say, things are looking up here, musta been connected to the lights.

[MUSIC NO. 14A – BLUE RAIN]

(*The sound of rain fills the room.*)

(*The* **JURORS** *take a quiet moment to retreat to their corners, watch the rain, and regroup with their thoughts.*)

(**NUMBER 9** *looks out the window;* **NUMBER 8** *looks out of the next window. As they watch the rain, privately.*)

NUMBER 9. We could be letting a killer go free.

NUMBER 8. Or we could be saving an innocent boy's life.

>(*The* **FOREMAN** *makes small talk with* **NUMBER 8**, *at the window.*)

FOREMAN. Wow! It's just pouring down rain. Reminds me of the storm we had last November, right in the middle of the Homecoming game. We're just starting to move the ball, and Boom! It starts to come down cats and dogs. In two minutes, it was mud practically up to your ass. We couldn't go nowhere. I swear, I almost bawled.

>(**NUMBER 8** *nods and smiles.*)

NUMBER 8. Sure is coming down.

>(*They look out at the rain.*)

>(**NUMBER 12** *breaks the ice with* **NUMBER 4**.)

NUMBER 12. Enjoying the summer? I mean, other than perhaps *today*, of course?

NUMBER 4. We try to take the girls out to Montauk every weekend. Have a sweet little boat, nothing grand, keeps me out of trouble. Do you sail? Looks like you soak up the sun. Your tan.

>(**NUMBER 12** *smiles awkwardly, shifts.*)

NUMBER 12. My tan?

NUMBER 4. (*Realizing his gaffe.*) Yes, no, of course, never mind.

NUMBER 12. No, I don't sail. Work, work, work. Too busy climbing that ladder.

NUMBER 4. Yes, of course.

>(**NUMBER 4** *goes to water cooler.*)

(**NUMBER 5** *and* **NUMBER 6** *talk in Spanish.*)

NUMBER 5. Aquí hay unos cuantos que se tienen que tranquilizar. (Some of these men need to calm down.)

NUMBER 6. Andale! Tu hablas español? (Oh, you speak Spanish?)

NUMBER 5. Un poquito... enough to get by.

NUMBER 6. I did not want to be on this case, I'm losing money every day. I got mouths to feed, you know?

NUMBER 5. My father told me to try and get off jury duty, but I thought maybe this one time...

NUMBER 6. The kid never had a chance, the defense lawyer was a joke.

NUMBER 5. This whole system's a joke, but you know, here we are.

NUMBER 6. Here we are.

> *(Most of the* **JURORS** *start to regroup at the table.* **NUMBER 7** *keeps to himself, losing patience with the deliberations.* **NUMBER 3** *re-enters from the bathroom, joins* **NUMBER 4** *at the water cooler.)*

> *(* **NUMBER 11** *adjusts his pocket-watch. Looks at the rain.)*

> *(* **NUMBER 12** *stands next to* **NUMBER 11** *at the windows.)*

NUMBER 12. That was pretty crazy, right? You know, at the agency, there are some pretty strange people; well, not strange, really, they just have peculiar ways of expressing themselves. Usually at the top of their lungs. It's probably the same in your business, bunch of crazies tearing it up full throttle, right? So, what do you do?

NUMBER 11. I'm a watchmaker.

>   *(Pause.)*

NUMBER 12. You must be very happy.

[MUSIC NO. 14 – RAINDROPS]

>   *(**NUMBER 12** moves away, then takes his place at the table.)*

>   *(**NUMBER 11** is lost in his memories as he watches the rain.)*

NUMBER 11.

RAINDROPS IN CONSTANT COLLISION
OFTEN PLAY TRICKS ON THE VISION.
FACES AND MEM'RIES ENTHRALLING,
BORNE ON THE FALLING RAIN.

YEARS IN THE HOUSE OF MY MOTHER
FADE ONE ON TOP OF THE OTHER...
EYES OF MY FATHER IMPLORING...
ASHES... AND POURING RAIN.

I NEVER SEE THEM AGAIN.
THERE IS NO END TO WHAT MEN WILL DO UNTO MEN...

SURE AS THE ATOMS ARE SPINNING,
NOW, JUST AS AT THE BEGINNING,
NATIONS WILL EVER BE WARRING,
SURE AS THE POURING RAIN.

>   *(Nearby, **NUMBER 6** gazes out the window.)*

NUMBER 6. Quite a case, right?

NUMBER 11. Quite a case, yes.

NUMBER 6. I mean, imagine killing your own father?

NUMBER 11. No, I cannot.

NUMBER 6. I love my papá.

NUMBER 11. As I loved mine.

NUMBER 6. Oh, what, he pass away or something?

NUMBER 11. Yes, something.

NUMBER 6. Damn shame.

NUMBER 11. You are fortunate you still have your father.

NUMBER 6. Well, he got sent back a few years ago. Papers and stuff.

NUMBER 11. Ah, yes, papers.

NUMBER 6. I miss him.

NUMBER 11. Yes, as do I.

> *(They look at the rain in silence, each again retreating to their private thoughts.)*

AND SO MY HEART,
IT KEEPS CALLING...
SURE AS THE FALLING RAIN.

> *(**NUMBER 10** joins **NUMBERS 3** and **4** at the water cooler.)*

NUMBER 10. *(Interrupting **NUMBER 11**.)* Well, isn't this the damndest thing you ever saw? Six to six. It's a joke.

NUMBER 3. What are we gonna do about it? Can't we break it somehow?

NUMBER 10. Those six bastards aren't going to change their minds.

NUMBER 4. Five of them already have changed their minds. There's no reason why they can't be persuaded to do it again.

NUMBER 7. *(Interrupting; over everybody.)* Okay, listen up now, here's what I think: We're goin' nowhere here. I'm ready to walk into court right now and declare a hung jury.

NUMBER 4. What?

NUMBER 10. There, you see?

NUMBER 3. Waitaminute you can't throw in the towel like that!

NUMBER 11. I'm not in favor of this.

NUMBER 4. Nor am I.

NUMBER 2. But you took an oath.

NUMBER 5. Doesn't your word mean anything?

NUMBER 7. It's a tie, six to six. We'll be at this all night.

NUMBER 11. So you'd rather quit than defend your opinion?

NUMBER 7. Sure, let the kid take his chances on twelve other guys with nothing to do.

NUMBER 9. Where is your self-respect?

NUMBER 7. *(To* **NUMBER 9**.*)* This whole game is rigged and you know it.

NUMBER 8. I don't think the court will accept a hung jury.

NUMBER 5. We haven't been in here very long.

       (The first and only time they agree:)

NUMBERS 3 & 8. He's right!

NUMBER 7. I'm not gonna change my mind.

NUMBER 6. I did.

NUMBER 2. I did.

NUMBER 5. So did I.

NUMBER 9. It's nothing to be ashamed of.

NUMBER 7. I'm not ashamed of nothin'.

NUMBER 5. You still don't think there's any room for reasonable doubt?

NUMBER 7. No, I don't.

NUMBER 11. Pardon, but perhaps you don't fully understand the term "reasonable doubt."

NUMBER 7. What d'ya mean, I don't understand it? I don't understand it?

NUMBER 11. Please –

NUMBER 7. How d'ya like this guy? The minute they swing open the camp gates, he comes over to this country running for his life and before he can even take a breath he's telling us how to run the show. The arrogance of this guy!

(**NUMBER 6** *rises, in defense of* **NUMBER 11.**)

FOREMAN. Come on...

NUMBER 6. *(To* **NUMBER 7.**) You mean you're calling him arrogant because he wasn't born here?

NUMBER 11. Please, please.

NUMBER 6. Well, I'm calling you arrogant because you are. How's that?

NUMBER 11. It doesn't matter.

NUMBER 7. *(Plowing on, at* **NUMBER 6.**) Look, sonny, nobody around here's gonna tell me what words I understand and what words I don't, especially some lousy foreigner. Because I'll knock his goddamn head off, understand?

(*The* **FOREMAN** *steps in between the men.*)

FOREMAN. Enough with the threats, already.

NUMBER 7. What, it's a figure of speech, right?

NUMBER 10. You can talk 'til your tongue is draggin' on the floor. The boy is guilty. Period, amen, know what I mean? Where's those cough drops, my friend?

NUMBER 2. They're all gone, *my friend.*

NUMBER 10. *(Under his breath.)* Yeah, what the hell good are ya?

NUMBER 7. Man, look at that rain.

NUMBER 9. There goes your ball game, son.

NUMBER 7. Good seats, too.

NUMBER 2. Say, could I see the knife for a second?

(The **FOREMAN** *gives the knife across the table to* **NUMBER 2,** *who opens and examines it.)*

FOREMAN. Here you go.

NUMBER 2. Thank you. Kind of creepy thinking where this has been. I mean *(He "plunges it.")* – gaaaak.

FOREMAN. Well, we're still tied up six-to-six. Who's got a suggestion?

NUMBER 12. I have. Let's get some dinner.

FOREMAN. Why don't we give it another hour.

NUMBER 12. Okay with me.

NUMBER 2. As long as we're stuck, there was this whole business about the stab wound and how it was made, the downward angle of it, you know?

NUMBER 3. Don't tell me we're gonna start with that. They went

[MUSIC NO. 15 – KILLING YOU]

OVER AND OVER AND OVER AND OVER IT.

NUMBER 2. And I don't go along with it. The boy is five-seven. His father was six-two. That's seven inches. I think it's a very awkward thing to stab down into the chest of someone who's more than half a foot taller than you.

NUMBER 3. Here, gimme that thing. Look, you're not gonna be satisfied 'til you see it again. I'm gonna give you a demonstration. Somebody get up.

> (*Pause.* **NUMBER 8** *rises and crosses to* **NUMBER 3**.)

> (*They stand looking at each other.*)

Okay.

SO IF I WAS GONNA KILL YA,
THERE COULD ONLY BE ONE WAY.

LISTEN UP THIS TIME,
'CAUSE LADIES, I'M
NOT DOIN' THIS ALL DAY.

I MAY BE SHORT, I GET IT,
BUT DON'T LET IT
GO TO YOUR HEAD:

SEE?

I FLIP MY GRIP,
THEN LET 'ER RIP...
AND YER DEAD!!

> (**NUMBER 3** *suddenly stabs downward, hard.*)

NUMBER 2. Look out!

> (*The blade stops an inch from* **NUMBER 8**'s *chest.*)

> (**NUMBER 8** *does not move;* **NUMBER 3** *smiles.*)

NUMBER 6.
> That's not
> funny.

NUMBER 5.
> What's the
> matter with
> you?

NUMBER 3.
> Oh, gimme a
> break. Nobody's
> hurt. Right?

NUMBER 8. No. Nobody's hurt.

NUMBER 3.

> ANYWAYS, THAT'S HOW HE'D KILL YA,
> I BEEN SAYIN' ALL ALONG.
>
> KEEP 'EM CLOTHED AND FED,
> YA WIND UP DEAD.
> NOW TELL ME WHERE I'M WRONG.

NUMBER 12. Down and in. I guess there's no argument.

NUMBER 5. Wait a minute.

> LET ME SEE THAT. HAND IT HERE.
> RESPECT IT. DON'T BE SO CAVALIER.
> I HATE THESE THINGS. BUT LET'S BE CLEAR…

(He closes the knife and holds it gingerly.)

> DO YOURSELF A FAVOR, WILLYA,
> AND AVOID THE STREETS UPTOWN,
>
> WHERE A FIVE-YEAR-OLD
> KNOWS HOW TO HOLD
> A KNIFE AND CUT YOU DOWN.

Funny, I wasn't thinking of it. I guess you try to forget those things.

> I WISH I WEREN'T SO FAMILIAR,
> BUT WHERE I'M FROM, IT'S NO JOKE.
>
> UNDERSTAND:
> IT'S *UNDERHAND,*

AND THEN EMPLOY AN UPWARD STROKE.

IT'S HOW THEY'RE USED, IT'S WHY THEY'RE MADE –

NUMBER 3.
DID YOU NOT HEAR WHAT I SAID?!

NUMBER 10. What a buncha mumbo jumbo! What's Anna May Wong gonna do, poke you with a chopstick?

FOREMAN. Show some respect!

> (**NUMBER 5** *confronts* **NUMBER 10**, *from the other side of the table.*)

NUMBER 5. I'd ram that chopstick in your eye, or your ear. Or I could just shove it up your fat, ignorant ass, know what I mean?

NUMBER 10. Fat? What's he talkin' about?

> (**NUMBER 5** *slams the table, fake "lunging" at* **NUMBER 10**, *who stumbles awkwardly in fear.*)

Keep him away from me!

> (*Several of the other men laugh at* **NUMBER 10**.)

FOREMAN. Quit yanking his chain!

NUMBER 10. It's a joke, you remember jokes? Jeez, no one has a sense of humor no more...

> (*Trailing off.*)

I SAY WHAT EV'RYBODY'S THINKIN'...

NUMBER 8. (*Ignoring him.*)
CONSIDER HIS HIST'RY WITH KNIVES, AND YOU WONDER.
I TEND TO AGREE WITH THE PRO.

NUMBER 5.
I TELL YOU, HE WOULD'VE ATTACKED HIM FROM UNDER.
THAT GASH DID NOT COME FROM BELOW.

NUMBER 3.

> *NO!!*

NUMBER 4. I don't think you can determine what type of wound this boy might or might not have made simply because he knows how to handle a knife.

NUMBER 3. That's right! That's absolutely right!

NUMBER 5. *(To* **NUMBER 3.***)*

> BUT IF I WERE GONNA KILL YOU,
> I KNOW WHAT I'D HAVE TO DO.

NUMBERS 3, 4 & 10.

> DOWN AND THEN IN.

NUMBERS 2, 6 & 11.

> NO, IT'S UP AND THEN UNDER!

NUMBER 8. *(To* **NUMBER 12.***)* What do you think? Is the boy guilty?

NUMBER 12. Well, uhm, I don't know...

NUMBERS 3, 4 & 10.

> DOWN AND THEN IN.

NUMBERS 2, 6 & 11.

> NO, IT'S UP AND THEN UNDER, AND...

> HE'S GUILTY!

> NOT GUILTY!

NUMBER 3. What d'ya mean you don't know?

NUMBER 12. I don't know.

NUMBERS 3, 4 & 10.

> HE'S GUILTY...

NUMBERS 2, 6 & 11.

> NOT GUILTY.

NUMBER 4. Just a minute. According to the woman across the street –

NUMBERS 3, 4 & 10.

> HE'S GUILTY!

NUMBERS 2, 6 & 11.

> NOT GUILTY!

NUMBER 7. *(Interrupting.)* Wanna know what I think? All this yakkity yak is getting us nowhere fast, just going over the same goddamn thing – tell you what, buddy, I'm gonna shake things up here. I'm changing my vote to "not guilty."

[MUSIC NO. 16 – STRIKE THREE]

NUMBER 3. No!

NUMBER 11. What?

NUMBER 3. He's guilty! Stand your ground!

NUMBER 7. You heard me. I've had enough.

NUMBER 11. No! That's no answer!

NUMBER 7. Hey, listen you, just worry about yourself.

NUMBER 11.
WHAT KIND OF MAN ARE YOU?
YOU VOTE "GUILTY" WITH EV'RYONE ELSE.

THEN, ONCE THE RAIN WASHES OUT THE BIG GAME,
YOU BACK DOWN WITH NO SHAME!

WELL, THAT'S UGLY, AND DARE
I SAY, MOST UNAMERICAN!

(He hits the table.)

OUR CONSTITUTION SAYS NOTHING ABOUT
"JUST LOOK OUT FOR YOURSELVES."

AND WHAT'S MORE, IN THE COUNTRY I FLED,
MEN WERE MINDLESSLY LED,
AND *YOU'D* LIKELY BE DEAD OVER THERE.

NUMBER 7. Listen, buddy –

NUMBER 11.
NO, YOU LISTEN, "BUDDY," YOU HAVE NO RIGHT!
THIS IS LIFE AND DEATH, NOT PLANS FOR THE NIGHT!
SO MUCH FOR ONE MAN TO BEAR:

NUMBER 11.
>ALL THIS TALK, THIS "YAKKITY YAK,"
>WITH YOUR LIFE OF LEISURE UNDER ATTACK.
>*MEIN GOTT!* DON'T YOU EVEN CARE...?!

NUMBER 7. *(Interrupting.)* Now, wait a minute. You can't talk like that to me!

NUMBER 11. I can talk like that to you. I can because it is my inalienable right! That is what makes this country great, and I will fight for that right even if you choose not to. If you want to vote "not guilty," then do it because you're convinced the boy is not guilty, not because you've had enough or because you're tired or because the game is starting! And if you think he is guilty, without a reasonable doubt, then vote that way!

NUMBER 11.
>WHERE IS YOUR
>   COURAGE?
>HOW DO YOU VOTE?

NUMBER 7.
>LISTEN HERE...

>HOW DO YOU VOTE?

>I ALREADY TOLD YOU...

>HOW DO YOU VOTE?!

>NOT... GUILTY.

>WHY?!

>I DON'T HAVE TO –

>YOU DO HAVE TO!
>SAY IT!

>NOT GUILTY.

>WHY?!

>BE... BECAUSE –

>WHY?!!

NUMBER 7. *(Cornered.)* Because I don't want to talk about it, alright?

(Quietly.) You don't get it.

*(Pause. **NUMBER 11** realizes that he does not, in fact, get it.)*

NUMBER 11. No. Perhaps I do not.

God help us.

NUMBER 12. *(Raising hand.)* I'd like to change my vote to "not guilty."

FOREMAN. *(Raising hand.)* Me too. "Not guilty."

[MUSIC NO. 17 – WHAT I MEANT]

NUMBER 10. Oh, Jesus H. Christ!

FOREMAN. Nine to three in favor of "not guilty."

NUMBER 10. What the hell is going on in this room?!

I DON'T UNDERSTAND YOU PEOPLE!
THIS SHIT IS OFF THE CHART!
GOD, EV'RY TIME YA TURN AROUND...

SOMEBODY ELSE IS TRYIN'
T' RIP THIS CASE APART.
BUT MEANWHILE, BACK HERE ON THE GROUND...

I'LL SAY IT: SURE, I HATE 'EM!

*(**NUMBER 6** turns away, angrily.)*

WAS I NOT CLEAR BEFORE?
THOUGHT WE WERE ALL IN ON THE JOKE.

I MUSTA BEEN TOO SUBTLE.
NO TIME FOR THAT NO MORE!
HOW'S THIS? I HOPE YOU BASTARDS CHOKE...!

*(**NUMBERS 2** and **7** turn away.)*

COME ON! YOU GIVE ME THE SHAFT?
WHEN SOME OF YA SAT THERE AND LAUGHED?
AND YOU KNEW WHAT I MEANT.

(**FOREMAN** *turns away.*)

FOREMAN. Ah, shaddup.

NUMBER 10.

THIS AIN'T NO TIME FOR TIDDLY-WINKIN':
WAKE UP! THE STATISTICS ARE OBSCENE!

THE REAL AMERICA'S BEEN SHRINKIN':

(**NUMBER 11** *turns away.*)

OUR MELTING POT'S ONE BIG LATRINE!

NUMBER 5. Knock it off!

NUMBER 10.

"THEY" FIGHT, THEN FUCK LIKE RATS,
AND CRANK OUT MORE SNOT-NOSE BRATS.

(**NUMBER 5** *turns away.*)

MURDER AND RAPE ARE JUST ROUTINE!
'CAUSE THEY'RE VIOLENT
AND IGNORANT:
WHAT A COMBINATION!

(**NUMBER 4** *looks away.*)

ADD INEBRIATION,
AND GET OUTTA THE WAY!

THEY COULD CONTRIBUTE, BUT THEY DON'T WANNA!

THEY TAKE WHAT ISN'T GIVEN
'CAUSE THE WORLD OWES 'EM A LIVIN',

AND IF WE DON'T ACT, *ADIOS, MAÑANA!*

(*To* **NUMBER 12.**)

WHATCHA LOOKIN' AT, BUTTERCUP?
IT'S ALL TRUE, AND YOU CAN LOOK IT UP.

(**NUMBER 12** *turns away.*)

WE ARE PAST THE LAST AND FINAL STRAW!
THAT'S IRREGARDLESS OF THE LAW!

I'VE KNOWN A COUPLA GOOD ONES,
BUT THEY'RE FEW AND FAR BETWEEN.

(**NUMBER 9** *turns away.*)

LOOK!
THEY'RE TAKIN' OVER! IT'S OUTRIGHT THEFT!
AND YOU'LL KNOW THAT I'M RIGHT WHEN THERE'S
    NOBODY LEFT!

THAT'S WHY JUSTICE IS JUST A MYTH.
LOOKIT ME. LOOK WHO I'M DEALIN' WITH!

(*Less singing than yelling now.*)

THIS AIN'T NO JURY OF *MY* PEERS,
BUT SPICS
AND SPOOKS
AND GOOKS
AND QUEERS!

(**NUMBER 8** *turns away.*)

THAT'S RIGHT!!

(*Individual instruments peel off and the band
falls away, as* **NUMBER 10***'s rant becomes
more hysterical and exposed.*)

FUCK ALL OF THIS!
FUCK ALL OF YOU!
(*Shouted in rhythm.*)
AND WHILE YOU'RE AT IT,
FUCK THE U.S.A., TOO!

(**NUMBER 3** *turns away.*)

NUMBER 10.
IT'S THE END OF THE WORLD!
THE GODDAMN END OF THE WORLD!
THEY'RE GONNA WIPE US OUT,
WHILE YOU ALL LET IT HAPPEN!
WE GOT THIS ONE; WE CAN'T LET HIM GO!

(More a <u>suggestion</u> *of rhythm by now.)*

NUMBER 2. *(Shouted in rhythm.)*
ENOUGH!
NOW, YOU JUST STOP ALL THIS.

NUMBER 10.
YOU WISE-ASS FAGGOT, YOU LITTLE PINK RAT!
WHAT I WOULDN'T GIVE FOR A BASEBALL BAT!
SAY IT AGAIN, AND I'LL KNOCK YOU FLAT SO FAST YOU
    WON'T EVEN KNOW WHAT –

*(***NUMBER 4*** rises, steps in front of* **NUMBER 10**
with a power and authority that stops
NUMBER 10 *in his tracks.)*

NUMBER 4. We've heard enough. Now sit down and keep your filthy mouth shut. Or I'll split your damned skull for you.

(With a cowed shudder, **NUMBER 10** *crosses to a chair and sits with his back to the men, who now regroup at the table.)*

(No one speaks for a moment.)

NUMBER 8. Nine of us think the boy is not guilty. We may be wrong. We may be right. We may save a young man's life. Or we may return a killer back to the streets. No one can really know for sure. But we have a reasonable doubt. No jury can declare a man guilty unless it's absolutely, resolutely sure. We nine can't understand how you three are still so sure. Maybe you can tell us.

NUMBER 4. Well, you've made some excellent points. But I still believe the boy is guilty. The woman across the street actually saw the murder being committed.

NUMBER 3. As far as I'm concerned, you can throw everything else out.

NUMBER 4. She said she kept tossing and turning, unable to sleep. At about ten minutes after twelve, she rolled over in bed and, looking out the window, saw the killing directly across the way through the windows of the passing el train. She says she got a good look at the boy in the act of stabbing his father, the "wrong" way. Frankly, I don't see how you can vote for acquittal.

NUMBER 12. *(Waffling.)* I'm changing my vote. I think he's guilty.

FOREMAN. You sure?

(**NUMBER 12** *nods his head "yes."*)

NUMBER 3. Good. Anybody else? Come on, the vote is eight to four.

NUMBER 11. What makes you consider one vote such a personal triumph?

NUMBER 3. I'm the competitive type.

(To all.) Okay. I think we're a hung jury. Let's take it inside to the judge.

NUMBER 4. You didn't want a hung jury before.

NUMBER 3. Yeah, well, now I do.

NUMBER 8. Let's go over it again.

NUMBER 3. We went over it again. *(About* **NUMBER 12.***)* Tony the Tiger over there is bouncing back and forth like a damn tennis ball.

NUMBER 12. Wait a second...

NUMBER 4. Maybe we can talk about setting some kind of a time limit at which we might begin to discuss the question of whether we're a hung jury or not.

> *(Removing and polishing his specs, **NUMBER 4** squints to see the clock.)*

The time is...

NUMBER 9. Quarter after six.

NUMBER 4. Quarter after six.

> *(**NUMBER 4** lays his specs on the table, tired. He clasps his fingers over the marks left by his spectacles at the sides of his nose.)*

NUMBER 9. *(To **NUMBER 4**.)* Don't you feel well?

NUMBER 4. I feel perfectly well, thank you.

(To others.) I was saying that seven o'clock would be a reasonable time to –

NUMBER 9. The reason I asked about that was because, well, you see, I couldn't help but notice you were –

NUMBER 4. I'm trying to settle something here. Do you mind?

NUMBER 9. I think this is important.

NUMBER 4. Very well.

NUMBER 9. Thank you. I'm sure you'll pardon me for this, but I was wondering why you were rubbing your nose like that?

NUMBER 3. Ah, come on, now, will ya please?

NUMBER 9. Right now, I happen to be talking to this gentleman here.

*(To **NUMBER 4**.)* Now, why were you rubbing your nose?

NUMBER 4. Well, if you must know, I was rubbing it because it bothers me a little.

NUMBER 9. I'm sorry. Is it because of your eyeglasses?

NUMBER 4. It is. Now, may we please get back to the case?

NUMBER 9. Your eyeglasses make those deep impressions on the sides of your nose. I hadn't noticed that before. They must be annoying.

NUMBER 4. They are very annoying.

NUMBER 9. I wouldn't know about that. I've never worn eyeglasses. Twenty-twenty.

NUMBER 4. We should all be so fortunate.

NUMBER 9. The woman who testified that she saw the killing had those same deep marks on the sides of her nose, though she wasn't wearing glasses during her testimony.

FOREMAN. I sat closest to her, she did have those marks on her nose.

NUMBER 2. I saw them, too!

NUMBER 11. She kept rubbing them in court.

NUMBER 9. Could those marks be made by anything other than eyeglasses?

NUMBER 4. No. No, they could not.

NUMBER 3. Listen, what are you saying here? I didn't see any marks.

NUMBER 4. I did.

NUMBER 8. Do you wear your eyeglasses when you go to bed?

NUMBER 4. No, I don't.

NUMBER 3. What does that matter, for Christ sakes!

NUMBER 4. No one wears eyeglasses to bed.

NUMBER 8. And she herself said that the murder took place just as she looked out and the lights went off a split second later.

(**NUMBER 4** *takes out a handkerchief, applies it to his sweaty brow.)*

NUMBER 3. So friggin' what?

NUMBER 8. So she couldn't have had time to put on her glasses.

NUMBER 3. That doesn't mean the boy didn't kill his father!

NUMBER 8. No, it means that the woman's eyesight is now in question.

NUMBER 4. I change my vote to "not guilty."

NUMBER 3. No! Why!

NUMBER 4. Because I now have reasonable doubt.

NUMBER 5. *(About the handkerchief.)* I thought you didn't sweat.

NUMBER 4. I didn't. Until now.

NUMBER 3. This is unbelievable. Are you men insane?

[MUSIC NO. 18 – THE ONLY ONE WHO SEES]

NUMBER 2. You can't send someone off to die on evidence like that.

NUMBER 3. Don't give me that crap!

NUMBER 8. Don't you think that the woman might have made a mistake?

NUMBER 3. No.

NUMBER 8. It's not possible?

NUMBER 3. No.

NUMBER 8. You don't think there's a possibility?

NUMBER 3. No.

NUMBER 8. There's no room for doubt?

NUMBER 3. No!

NUMBER 12. Yes.

NUMBER 3. What?

NUMBER 12. I'm changing my vote back to "not guilty."

NUMBER 8. *(To* **NUMBER 10.***)* Do you still think he's guilty?

NUMBER 10. Yes, I think he's guilty. But I couldn't care less.

NUMBER 8. How do you vote?

NUMBER 10. "Not guilty." You smart bastards do whatever you want.

NUMBER 3. You're the worst son of a bitch... I think he's guilty.

NUMBER 8. Does anyone else think he's guilty?

NUMBER 4. No.

NUMBER 3. You're all a buncha friggin' –

NUMBER 9. It's eleven-to-one.

NUMBER 8. *(To* **NUMBER 3.***)* You're alone.

NUMBER 3. I don't care, I say he's guilty, what else do you want?

NUMBER 8. We want your arguments.

NUMBER 3. I gave you all my arguments.

NUMBER 8. We want to hear them again. We have as much time as it takes.

NUMBER 3. Everything – every single thing that came out in that courtroom, but I mean everything, says he's guilty.

NUMBER 9. We disagree.

NUMBER 3. Do you think I'm an idiot or something?

FOREMAN. No, we just think you're wrong.

NUMBER 3. I'm entitled to my opinion.

NUMBER 2. So convince us.

NUMBER 3. Why don'tcha take that stuff about the old man, the old man who lived there, and heard everything.

NUMBER 6. Not with the el train passing by.

NUMBER 3. The old man saw him. Right there on the stairs.

NUMBER 2. He couldn't have made it to the door in fifteen seconds.

NUMBER 12. We proved that.

NUMBER 3. What's the difference how many seconds it took? What's the difference?

NUMBER 9. It's the difference between life and death.

NUMBER 3. I'm telling you every single thing that went on has been twisted and turned in here. The knife falling through a hole in his pocket?

NUMBER 5. A hundred guys could've had the same knife.

NUMBER 3. That whole thing about hearing the boy yell? The phrase was "I'm gonna kill you."

FOREMAN & NUMBER 6.
BEING A FATHER...

NUMBER 3. That's what he said. To his own father.

NUMBER 7. You said the same thing to him. *(Referring to* **NUMBER 8.***)*

NUMBER 3. *(Sputtering out.)* I don't care what I said!

NUMBERS 9, 10 & 11.
...TOO EASY AT ALL...

NUMBERS 2, 4 & 7.
...AT ALL...

NUMBER 3. It was his father. My God, don't you see? How come I'm the only one who sees? I can feel that knife going in –

> (**NUMBER 3**'s *rage is consumed by the painful memory of the fight with his son.*)

NUMBER 9. It's not your son on trial.

> (*The others are silent.*)

> (**NUMBER 3** *sputters, exhausted.*)

NUMBER 8. It's up to us, all of us, to think clearly, without anger, without prejudice. A young boy's life is in our hands.

[MUSIC NO. 19 – HOPEFULLY NOT TOO LATE]

A SUDDEN STORM DUMPS ALL ITS RAIN,
AND FOLKS COMPLAIN
FROM THE BRONX TO DOWNTOWN.

BUT THAT TINY STREAM THAT PERSEVERES
FOR A MILLION YEARS
WEARS A MOUNTAIN DOWN.

AND THAT'S THE WHOLE IDEA, FELLA –
SO SIMPLE, YET SUBLIME.
THROUGH LESS EXPLOSION,
MORE EROSION:
PROGRESS AND TIME TAKE TIME.

JURORS.

THOSE DINOSAURS ROAMED WORLDWIDE,   OOH.
UNTIL THEY DIED.
AND THOUGH NO ONE KNOWS HOW,

CONSIDER THIS – HAD THEY ALL SURVIVED,
HELD ON AND THRIVED,
WHERE WOULD WE BE NOW?

NUMBER 8.
> AND THAT'S THE BIG IDEA, FELLA –
> THE UNIVERSE WON'T WAIT.
> AVOID THE LOT THAT TIME FORGOT,
> AND HOPE THAT YOU'RE NOT TOO LATE.
>
> HISTORY SHOWS US, EVER SINCE THE DAWN OF MAN,
> MINISCULE ADVANCES ON OUR WAY
>
> HELP CHANGE THE MEANING OF "WE DO THE BEST WE CAN"
> EV'RY GENERATION...

	JURORS.
THAT'S THE WHOLE IDEA!	AH...
ISN'T IT?	
WHY HUMANS PROCREATE?	
TO THINK, WE MIGHT	OOH,
JUST GET THIS RIGHT!	AH...!
BUT HOPEFULLY NOT TOO	
LATE.	
	THAT'S THE BIG IDEA...
FORGET YOUR PRIDE:	
	THAT'S THE BIG IDEA...
REACH DEEP INSIDE.	

SOLO JURORS. *(Variously.)*

NOT GUILTY.	THAT'S THE BIG IDEA...
NOT GUILTY.	

NUMBER 8.
> WE'RE HERE, WE'RE GONE

SOLO JURORS. *(Variously.)*

NOT GUILTY.	THAT'S THE BIG IDEA...
NOT GUILTY.	

NUMBER 8.
> AND LIFE GOES ON.

SOLO JURORS. *(Variously.)* **JURORS GROUP 1.**

NOT GUILTY.	THAT'S THE BIG IDEA...
NOT GUILTY.	

NUMBER 8.
SO WHEN WE'RE DONE,

SOLO JURORS. *(Variously.)*
NOT GUILTY.
NOT GUILTY.

NUMBER 8.
GO CALL YOUR SON.

SOLO JURORS. *(Variously.)*
NOT GUILTY.
NOT GUILTY.

JURORS GROUP 2. *(Joining.)*
THAT'S THE BIG IDEA...

A FEW JURORS. *(Joining.)*
HOPEFULLY NOT...

JURORS GROUP 2.
HOPEFULLY NOT TOO LATE.

JURORS GROUP 1.
THAT'S THE BIG IDEA...

JURORS GROUP 2.
HOPEFULLY NOT TOO LATE.

JURORS GROUP 1.
THAT'S THE BIG IDEA...

(Some raw nerve inside **NUMBER 3** *uncoils, loosens; something releases deep inside him.)*

NUMBER 3.
...NOT GUILTY...

*(***NUMBER 3** *sits in his seat, beaten, head in hand.)*

(The **JURORS** *take a breath, having reached a verdict.)*

(The **FOREMAN** *moves to the door and knocks on it; the unseen guard opens it.)*

FOREMAN. We have a verdict. *(Looking back at the other* **JURORS.***)* Give us a minute, please.

*(***FOREMAN** *offers* **NUMBER 3** *a clean white handkerchief, which he accepts.)*

[MUSIC NO. 20 – EVENSONG]

(The **FOREMAN** *and the* **OTHERS** *gather their things from around the room, and take their places back in the jury box. Only* **NUMBER 3** *and* **NUMBER 8** *are still in the room;* **NUMBER 3** *remains seated at the table.)*

FOREMAN.
THE SKY GROWS CLEAR...

NUMBER 2.
THE LIGHT IS FAIR...

NUMBER 12.
A BREEZE THAT RIPPLES...   **NUMBERS 2 & 4.**
                                                    BREATH...
...THE AIR...

*(***NUMBER 6** *and* **NUMBER 11** *share a brief smile as they leave.)*

NUMBERS 2, 4 & 12.
...A MISTY VEIL

NUMBERS 2, 4, 5 & 12.
THAT SLOWLY RISES AND...

NUMBERS 2, 4, 5, 10 & 12.
HOLDS...

*(***NUMBER 7** *allows* **NUMBER 9** *to pass before him.)*

NUMBERS 10 & 12.
AND THE WORLD IS NOT BRAND NEW,

NUMBERS 7 & 9.
AS IT MUSCLES TOWARD FORGET...

NUMBERS 2, 5, 6, 10 & 12.
AND THE CITY'S NOT REBORN.

NUMBERS 4, 7, 9 & 11.
IT'S ONLY WET.

NUMBER 6.
AND YET...

NUMBER 11.
AND YET...

*(****NUMBER 8**** gets the one remaining jacket from the rack.)*

*(He stands behind ****NUMBER 3****, holding the jacket up. ****NUMBER 3**** rises, allows ****NUMBER 8**** to help him into it.)*

ALL (EXCEPT NUMBERS 3 & 8).
HER SKYLINE SHRUGS,

AND CLAWS,
AND SMILES...

DIVINE AND
CHEAP.

NUMBER 8. I'm Louis.

NUMBER 3. Harry.

*(They shake hands, tentatively. ****NUMBER 8**** lets ****NUMBER 3**** exit first, who joins the others.)*

ALL (EXCEPT NUMBER 8).
A CRUSH OF SOLITUDE –

NUMBER 2.
GEARS GRIND...

NUMBER 11.
A SIREN...

NUMBER 7.
A BABY CRIES...

NUMBER 12.
WITH CREAK AND RUMBLE,
EVENTIDE UNFOLDS.

OTHERS.
OH...

*(****NUMBER 8**** leaves, joins the others in the jury box.)*

ALL.
> O GASEOUS MAW OF SUMMER!
> STENCH AND RUST,
> GOLDEN DUST...
>
> AS LIGHTS BLINK UP,
> A SCARLET SUN
>
> WHISPERS
>
> SLEEP,
>
> SLEEP.

> *(Lights fade to black.)*

The End